CAT TALES 2:
Fantastic Feline Fiction

In the Same Series:

Cat Tales, edited by George H. Scithers

CAT TALES 2:
Fantastic Feline Fiction

Edited by George H. Scithers

Cover illustration by David Palumbo

Interior illustrations by George Barr

WILDSIDE PRESS

CAT TALES 2: FANTASTIC FELINE FICTION

ISBN 1-4344-0912-0

Compilation © 2010 by Wildside Press

Wildside Press
WWW.WILDSIDEPRESS.COM

CONTENTS

INTRODUCTION

by George H. Scithers

In this, the second *Cat Tales* anthology, we present fourteen stories, one essay, two haiku, and three other poems, all involving cats. Only one classic story this time: "Mrrrar!" by the late Edgar Pangborn, and of course H.P. Lovecraft's "Cats and Dogs" is a classic essay. The rest are freshly written: seven fantasies, including a deal with a devil that turns out rather differently than the one in our previous issue, the first *Cat Tales*; three crime & mystery stories; and a few that don't fit into any convenient category, but prefer to be like cats — and walk alone through our pages. 🐾

IF WISHES WERE FISHES

by P.D. Cacek

IF THE MOTH had coöperated and simply allowed itself to be caught and eaten when it first drifted through the tear in the screen door, the redecoration of the family room, hallway, and parlor would not have been necessary.

Or quite so extensive.

Twitching a thread from the remains of a tatted doily that had, according to family history, once belonged to the wife of some famous father-of-his-country or some such nonsense, Stacpoole furrowed the small black patch between his ears and swept the shadowed, and momentarily tidy, den with his peeled-onion-colored eyes.

He'd been only one or two swats away from snatching the white-winged little invader when it suddenly changed direction in a blatant kamikaze attack. The offense to his dignity had been so unexpected it had literally turned him tail over nose.

And into the wall.

And the plant stand.

And a small occasional table.

He would, however, not take any responsibility for the brass funeral bowl that turned convex to concave after its fall.

That was the moth's fault.

Eyes narrowing to feign indifference, Stacpoole

lifted his left front paw and began to lick the fur smooth. Moths were incredibly easy to fool.

Given enough time.

And talent for pantomime.

Yawning just long enough to make it sound realistic, Stacpoole curled himself into a little black-and-white ball (that never failed to produce cooing and *ah* sounds from his two-legged food-providers) and closed his eyes.

To mere slits.

It only took a moment for the moth to think it was safe (*foolish creature*) and flutter away from its hiding place on the white lampshade.

And a moment after that, Stacpoole became a moth-seeking missile mere seconds away from contact.

If only the moth hadn't *zigged* when it should have *zagged*.

The lampshade, lamp, and Stacpoole hit the floor at almost the same time — one crumbling, one shattering, and one landing on its feet with indignant disdain — while the moth fluttered out of the room.

Stacpoole sat down to wash the tension from his whiskers and plan his revenge when a cloud of pink smoke slowly began to curl out of the broken lamp.

It was very curious . . . but since he was a cat and had long heard what curiosity could do to his kind, he ignored it.

Until —

"Uh, excuse me?"

Stacpoole looked up and felt his tongue stop in mid-lick. The food-provider was *male*, bare-chested and dark of hair and eyes . . . but where Stacpoole's human had two legs, this one hovered above the floor on the column of thick, pink smoke.

Very curious, indeed.

"Did you see who broke the lamp?"

Stacpoole pulled his tongue in and blinked.

"Oh . . . *you* broke it?"

Stacpoole blinked again.

"Wow, this is a new one." The odd, half-smoke food-provider ran a pale hand through his hair and exhaled loudly. "I don't think I've ever heard about something like this happening, but . . . rules are rules, I guess."

The smoky food-provider folded his arms, one over the other and nodded.

"I AM THE GENIE OF THE LAMP!"

Stacpoole cringed beneath the thundering voice as every black-and-white hair on his body went on point.

"Oh," the half-human said, his voice dropping to a more agreeable level, "sorry. I've been in that lamp for so long, I got carried away."

Stacpoole accepted the apology and sat back on his haunches.

"Anyway, I'm authorized by the Grand Genie of Annobandah to present you with three wishes . . . but considering you're . . . you know, a cat . . ."

Stacpoole straightened an errant whisker.

"Right. This isn't going to be easy, but . . . I know, how 'bout I give you one wish. Anything you want. How's that?"

Stacpoole watched the funnel end of the smoke curl and weave across the floor.

"You like milk? Or maybe cream? How would you like a *swimming pool* filled with fresh cream?"

Stacpoole yawned.

"No. Okay, how about a solid gold scratching pole? No, wait, that wouldn't work. A wall-to-wall litter box? Twenty-four hour tummy rubber? I know . . . *fish!* How about I provide you with all the fish in the wor—"

A tiny movement caught Stacpoole's eye, and he saw the moth flutter past the den's open door. Business called. Chin to the floor, tail trembling in anticipation, he made ready, set, and darted straight through the half-man's pink smoke. Bounded out through the open door.

"No — *wait!* Come back here, you mangy feline! Don't you know what I am? I'm a *genie*, and I can give you your greatest wish . . . *are you listening to me?*"

Behind him, something began to make a sucking noise, but since he knew he wasn't responsible for it, Stacpoole kept his attention fixed on the moth.

"I don't believe this!" The half-man's voice echoed outward from the den. "I've been stuck in that lousy

IF WISHES WERE FISHES

lamp for fifteen centuries, and what happens? *A cat lets me out?* It's *not fair!* I have to grant a wish! I know my rights! I deserve my freedom! If I don't grant a wish — *no! I've been robbed! No-o-o-o!"*

As he snatched the moth out of the air, Stacpoole heard a moan from the other room — a moan strangely similar to those his food-provider made when he woke in the morning to find half a mouse in his slipper.

Holding his fluttering trophy gently so he wouldn't crush it, Stacpoole trotted back to the den just as the half-man dissolved into a pillar of smoke and disappeared back into the shattered lamp, which neatly reassembled itself and landed on the end-table again.

The moth was only a bit worse for wear when Stacpoole spat it out. Hopping stiff-legged up to the lamp, he sat down and huffed. Indignant.

How rude, he thought to himself. *You'd think after fifteen centuries he would have had a bit more patience.* 🐾

The author tells us, "Our publisher, John Betancourt, showed me a painting (the cover of this anthology) and said, 'Trish, write a story.' (I work best under extreme pressure.)

"I have a story out from a Scholastic Books anthology, 666 — The Sign of the Beast, have a new ghost collection coming out soon from Prime Books, and am currently working on a new novel."

A CAT'S WISH . . .

If wishes were fishes
Then all cats would dine
On tureen of flounder
And mulberry wine.

— P.D. Cacek

THE CASE OF THE UNFORTUNATE MRS RIPLEY'S CAT

by Jeff Crook

Sunday MORNING found my friend Mr Sherlock Holmes absent from our old quarters at 221B Baker Street. This was not unusual, as Holmes rarely frequented his rooms when deeply involved in a case. I settled down at the table to await his return, with Holmes's untouched breakfast before me and a stack of newspapers at my elbow.

A few hours later, the room was growing rather close and hot. The season was unusually warm and it had not rained in almost two weeks, so the extreme dustiness of the streets forbade the opening of windows to let in a breath of air. I had finished the last newspaper and found little of interest, and was just beginning to consider a visit to my club, when I heard Holmes's familiar tread upon the stair. To my utter surprise, he called from without, "Watson, how are you?" The door swung open and he bounded into the room, only to freeze in horror upon the threshold.

"Watson, what is *that*?" he hissed.

"It's a cat, Holmes," I said of the ball of black and white patches snoozing in my lap.

He snatched the handkerchief from his top pocket and pressed it to his nose. "Watson, as a medical man you should know better than anyone the effects of *cat hair* upon a delicate respiratory system."

"Delicate respiratory system?" My laughter woke our feline visitor. She rose, stretched and poured out of my lap onto the floor. Holmes leaped into his favourite old chair and sat curled up upon his long legs. I said, "My dear fellow, any man who can inhale the poisonous atmospheres this room has harboured over the years isn't likely to be overcome by a few cat hairs."

"Nevertheless, I *detest* cats. Get rid of it, Watson," he said with a sneeze.

"Very well," I said. The cat followed me to the door, which I opened. It peered into the hall for a moment, then leaped onto the settee and settled sphinx-like atop yesterday's *Pall Mall Gazette,* facing my friend and sleepily blinking her pale yellow eyes.

"I think she likes you, Holmes," I said and closed the door. "By the way, how did you know . . . ?"

"The smell of your . . . ah, cigarette smoke is . . . ah, unmistakable!" He sneezed again. The cat unfolded one paw and began to methodically lick its pads. "Wherever did the beast come from?" he said, obviously annoyed by the scratching noise of her tongue.

"It followed Mrs Hudson when she came to collect your breakfast dishes," I said. "By the way, I hope you don't mind, but I . . ."

"Not at all. You know how my appetite goes at times like these."

"You have a case then?" I asked.

He waved his handkerchief distractedly, then clapped it once more to his nose. "It's more gruesome than interesting. Nothing to especially recommend it."

"What is it?"

"Oh, Bradstreet called me over to examine a torso found in a trunk floating down the Thames."

"Just the torso?" I asked. Holmes's appallingly casual discussion of the most horrific crimes sometimes bordered on callousness, but only because he couldn't allow ordinary human sensibilities to interfere with his observations.

"They're combing both shores for the rest of the body," he said as he glared at the cat. She nibbled at the underside of her paw, tugging at the fur between the pads. "Though I doubt they'll find anything. The trunk was locked. I suspect it's an altogether common murder, though certainly brutal enough to cause a sensation in the press, once the particulars are revealed. Likely it will be solved via the usual police methods. Watson, I believe your friend may be injured."

"My friend?"

"Your cat. It is worrying at its right forepaw."

I knelt beside the settee and scratched her between her black ears. She was tolerant of my ministrations, an altogether admirable patient, unlike some. The fur around the pads of her paw was matted with some dark material that resisted my efforts to remove. Using a pair of surgical scissors, I trimmed a knot from between the pads which surely must have been most uncomfortable for her.

It was a curious substance that she had stepped in, neither as thick as paint nor as dark as asphalt. "Holmes, I believe this is dried blood," I said, though I could find no injury to her paw.

"Indeed?" he said with eyebrows raised. He rose from his chair and circled the room, keeping as much distance between himself and the cat as the furnishings allowed, until he reached the door. Opening it, he called down, "Mrs Hudson!"

"Do you think we might test it using your method?" I asked, recalling the first time I met Holmes. He had just discovered a chemical reagent precipitated by hæmoglobin. Holmes's method for detecting the presence of blood had proven quite useful on several cases.

But before he could answer, our dear old landlady appeared at the door quite out of breath. "Yes, Mr Holmes?" she wheezed.

"Mrs Hudson, does this creature belong to you?"

"No sir, he belongs to you, from what I can tell," she said.

"Mrs Hudson, please," Holmes sighed.

"Oh, you mean the cat. I thought you meant the doctor," she said with a wink in my direction. "No sir, Mr Holmes, she belongs to Dr Ripley."

"The dentist who lives above the tobacconist's shop on the corner?" I said.

"The very one. She's been moping around my door for three days now. Poor thing, I fed her a saucer of milk; and now I cannot persuade her to go home."

"Thank you, Mrs Hudson," Holmes said and closed the door. "Are you acquainted with Dr Ripley?" he asked.

"I've never met the man, but I have seen his plaque beside the door."

"Well done, Watson," Holmes smiled. "Come. I am in need of a cigarette."

"Would you like one of mine?" I said, reaching for my cigarette case.

"No, let us visit the tobacconist's shop on the corner," he said on his way out the door. I paused only to grab my hat. "And do bring the cat," Holmes shouted up the stairs. I retrieved her from the settee and caught up with Holmes at the door to Baker Street. A cloud of dust blew in as we stepped outside. He set off at once at a terrific pace, and it was all I could do to keep up without losing my hold on the cat. The creature was positively terrified by the passing carriages and the shouting of the newsboys. I deduced that this was no alley creature. She was used to being safely indoors.

WE WERE both glad to enter the cool calm of the tobacconist's shop.

"Marley, old man, how have you been keeping?" Holmes inquired.

The proprietor, an elderly gentleman of that name, looked up from his newspaper and smiled his toothless smile. "Good afternoon, Mr Holmes. And to you as well, Dr Watson," Marley said. I touched my hat. "Your usual, Mr Holmes?"

"Please."

"I see you've found Dr Ripley's cat," Marley said as he set a box of cigarettes on the counter.

"Is he the one to whom it belongs?" Holmes said, as though surprised.

"Indeed, sir."

"And how is your tenant?"

"He keeps to himself, sir. Him and his wife. Of course, she's ill with something or other."

"Is it serious?" I asked.

"From what I can tell, rather serious indeed," he said with a sad nod of his head.

"And his practice?" Holmes asked.

"I don't believe he has any practice at all, if you take my meaning."

"No patients?" I asked.

"Not that I've ever seen." The old man collected the money Holmes had placed on the counter and returned his change. "His wife has a small income left to her by her father, so Dr Ripley doesn't need to work, it seems."

"What does he do, then?" Holmes asked.

"He keeps orchids, sir. In my old hothouse out back. He's quite mad about them, actually. He's not a very talkative man, positively morose, you might say, but you get him on the subject of horticulture and you'll get a right earful."

"The hothouse out back, you say?" Holmes said. "May I?"

"Be my guest, Mr Holmes. Only don't touch any of his pretty flowers, not if you value your life."

We passed out of the shop and into a short, dark hall, at the end of which was a staircase and a glass-paned door glowing with sunlight. Through this door we proceeded into a narrow, well-kept garden with a small greenhouse taking up one end, the panes of which were almost entirely fogged.

Holmes paused on the doorstep to take in the surroundings, then set off down the side of the path with his eyes fixed to the ground.

I lowered Dr Ripley's cat to the steps. "Here we are then, girl. Home at last," I said. She shot straight across the garden and curled herself around Holmes's legs.

I joined them in front of the greenhouse. Holmes rattled a large padlock that was fixed to the door. "This appears new," he said, then pressed his face against the glass. "It looks positively tropical in there, Watson." He seemed finally to notice the cat and produced a loud sneeze.

I squinted through the glass, trying to see through the moisture clinging to the windows. The vent above the door was closed tight. I could see little of interest other than several dozen pots lining the shelves, and a potting bench atop which lay a pair of gloves, an ordinary pair of gardening shears, a bag of pebbles, and a pruning saw. The floor, however, was heaped with scattered mounds of fresh soil.

"Peat, surely. The man does grow orchids," Holmes remarked of my observation. "Though I can't imagine why he would need lime." He pointed out a bag of white powder under the bench.

"Holmes," I said as I peered through the glass. "Where are his orchids?" Every pot in the hothouse appeared empty of any growth.

"Where, indeed," Holmes said darkly, then turned. "Dr Ripley, I presume?"

"This is private property," said the man who had come up behind us, silent as a panther. He was not a tall man, nor especially rotund, but there was something utterly grotesque about his features, as though nothing about him were in its proper proportions. It was little wonder Dr Ripley had no patients, for who would submit to having his teeth pulled by such a great troll of a man.

"I have permission from the landlord. My name is Sherlock Holmes."

"What business do you have here, Mr Holmes?"

"We are returning your cat," Holmes said. He gestured at the animal crouched in terror at my feet.

"That's not my cat," Ripley said.

"Ah! There you are, Watson. You can't believe everything people tell you."

"She belonged to my wife," Ripley said.

"Belonged?" Holmes asked.

"My wife has gone home to live with her mother," Ripley said, then added with a sinister squint, "To India."

"Oh well, perhaps Mrs Hudson will keep her," said Holmes with a shrug. "I was also hoping to be allowed to view your orchids," he added.

"My orchids?" the man said. He seemed to crouch, as though about to run, or perhaps spring, like a tiger digging its claws into the soil. "Why do you want to see my orchids?

"I understand your *Phalænopsis equestris* are of the very best quality. I am something of an orchid fancier myself, but my friend Dr Watson utterly detests them."

"He does, does he?" Dr Ripley turned his queer and angry visage upon me. "Pray, sir, what is the matter with orchids?" he said.

"Nothing at all," I said. "I merely prefer roses." I didn't like the way this strange brute had imposed himself between us and the only exit from the garden. I brushed by him to be nearer the door. He turned with me as I passed, his great hands clenching and unclenching as though he wished to wrap his fingers around my throat. Behind him, Holmes stooped down to examine something in front of the hothouse door.

"Roses!" Ripley snorted with the disdain of a true connoisseur and showed me his back, which had something of a hunch on the left side. Holmes stood quickly, a smile of triumph upon his face.

Ripley said, "You may not see my orchids, Mr Holmes. They are not for public display; and, I repeat, this is private property." He lunged suddenly and snatched up the terrified cat by the scruff of its neck. She yowled most ferociously and writhed in his fist with her tiny claws extended. Ripley thrust her into my arms. "And take this beast with you. I want nothing to do with anything that belonged to my cursed wife." The poor creature clung to me in her terror.

"Off to India," Holmes said in a friendly fashion and **tsk**ed sympathetically. "Perhaps it's for the best. In any case, I was led to believe your wife was rather ill."

"She's not," Ripley said. "Though I can't say as I wish she weren't."

"Then the laudanum belongs to you?" Holmes asked.

"What laudanum?"

"The bottle sitting in your upstairs window, behind the curtain."

Dr Ripley turned to the window in surprise, then his face drained of colour. "Well, yes. My wife used laudanum, but not for medicinal reasons." He had gone, in one instant, from an angry to a broken man. I had never seen so swift a decline. I thought he might crumble before us.

"I see," Holmes sighed. "Well Watson, since we cannot view Dr Ripley's orchids, I believe it is now a matter for the police."

"The police!" Ripley shrieked. He wrung his hands, eyes darting around in terror. "What do you want with the police? They're my orchids. I didn't steal them."

"Of course you didn't steal them," Holmes said. "But I believe Inspector Bradstreet will be most fascinated by the bloody paw print here upon the doorstep." He pointed at a dark brown smudge by his shoe. With a beastly howl, Dr Ripley lunged past me and entered the house.

"Watson!" Holmes shouted as he raced by me in pursuit. I followed as best I could, but was hampered by the terrified cat clinging to my waistcoat. At the top of the stairs, I found Holmes furiously rattling the knob of a closed door. Marley appeared at the bottom of the stairs shouting what was the matter.

"Summon the police at once!" Holmes cried and threw his shoulder against the door. It gave with a mighty crash. Holmes leapt into the room only to find it empty. A reclining chair stood by the window, and leaning over it a motorized drilling contraption like some kind of gigantic metal insect. Those shelves not lined with books held dusty old boxes of Dr Ripley's blend of dentifrice. Holmes hurried to the next door and found it locked as well.

"Watson, put down that blasted cat and help me!" he cried.

"I'm trying," I said. Each time I managed to extract one claw, she would latch on with another. Holmes hardly needed my help anyway, as with one thrust he burst the door almost from its hinges.

"Now, now, none of that!" Holmes shouted as he rushed into the room. I heard Dr Ripley give a terrific shriek of despair, followed by a crash of glass.

"Holmes!" I shouted and ran to the aid of my friend, having finally extracted myself from the cat. As I entered the room, Dr Ripley thrust by me with his ape-like arms. But it was not yet so many years since I had trod the rugby fields of Blackheath. I was close upon his shirt tails, which had come out during his struggle with Holmes, before he was even through the door.

Holmes himself was not far behind me, and the three of us crossed the small dental surgery as close as dancers at a ball. I had the man almost in my grasp when, out of nowhere, the cat appeared, apparently as desperate to flee the room as her former master. As she darted between Ripley's feet, he stumbled and with an angry shout plummeted headfirst down the stairs. He came to a sudden and sickening stop at the bottom, with his chin resting upon his shoulder and his neck bent at an angle that left no doubt as to his fate.

"Well, Watson, he got what he wanted," Holmes said. "Pardon me, I believe I feel faint." He sagged against the wall. I caught him just before he slipped to the floor.

"My God, Holmes, you're soaked with ether!" I exclaimed.

"Is that what it is?" he laughed weakly.

"You've got to get out of these clothes," I said as I helped him off with his coat. I led him into the garden and lowered him onto a stack of old bricks beside the door.

After several tense moments, in which I feared that Holmes might lose consciousness, the fresher air roused him and some of the color returned to his damp, drawn face. I unbuttoned his collar and examined the bump on his head. There were bits of glass in his hair.

"I don't think it's serious," I said.

"Thank you, Doctor. I stopped the fool from drinking a bottle of ether, so he broke it over my head."

"He was trying to kill himself?" I asked.

"He succeeded," Holmes said.

"But why?"

"Because he murdered his wife, Watson. Murdered her and buried her, or parts of her, anyway, in Marley's hothouse."

AN HOUR LATER found us back once more in the sitting room at Baker Street. Revived by a glass of brandy and a change of clothes, Holmes was his usual restless self, pacing about, scanning the newspapers, already turning his keen intellect in search of another problem to solve. I sat at my old desk by the door, jotting down notes on the case, while Ripley's cat was once more curled upon my lap, purring contentedly. Inspector Bradstreet had joined us, smiling like the cat who ate the canary.

"Well, if you ask me, this has been an altogether untidy business, Mr Holmes," Bradstreet chuckled. "To think a monster like Dr Ripley could commit so heinous a crime, why, almost before your very nose."

Holmes tossed aside the newspaper and collapsed into his armchair.

"What's to become of the cat?" Bradstreet asked me.

"Mrs Hudson offered to keep her, but Holmes would not hear of it. So I will take her home to my wife," I said. "She has been asking me for a cat."

"To think Dr Ripley must have also loved his wife, once upon a time," Holmes yawned.

"He had an odd way of showing it," Bradstreet said. "The woman was gravely ill, a tumor of the brain, which left her demented and quite violent, according to the neighbors. Ripley drugged her with laudanum to keep her quiet, but sometimes her mania overcame the effects of the opium. They had several terrific rows that resulted in the police being summoned."

"Most likely he administered an overdose which killed her," I said.

"An admirable deduction, Watson, but I do not think it very likely," Holmes said.

"What is your theory?" I asked.

"Well, if he had poisoned her with laudanum, he might have claimed she poisoned herself. Who would contradict him?" He drummed his fingers on the arm of the chair. "No, her death must have been a violent and sudden one. Why else go to such elaborate lengths to dispose of her body?"

"Yes, but whether he killed her by accident or design, we'll never know," Bradstreet said.

"Thanks to the unfortunate Mrs Ripley's cat," Holmes said.

She rested her chin on my knee and sighed.

"What I'd like to know, Mr Holmes," Bradstreet said, "is how you made the connection between the torso in the river and Dr Ripley's wife."

"I didn't," Holmes sullenly said.

At Bradstreet's puzzled expression, I offered an explanation. "It was the cat. She had blood on her paw."

"She might have come by that anywhere," Bradstreet said. "Ripley was a dentist, after all. She might have stepped in a drop of blood from one his patients."

"Dr Ripley had no patients," I said.

"A cat with a bloody paw is sure to leave bloody paw prints. I simply looked for them. It hasn't rained for days upon days. When I found one upon the hothouse doorstep, it left no doubt that some horrible deed had been committed behind its fogged panes," Holmes said.

"Oh, I see! Yes, it makes perfect sense now," Bradstreet exclaimed. "I say, that's quite extraordinary."

"It's nothing of the kind," Holmes said. "It was sheer luck. You might have done as well yourself, Bradstreet, had you been in possession of the cat."

"You're very kind to say so, Mr Holmes."

"There was also the new padlock," Holmes continued. "I believe Dr Ripley installed it to keep the cat out of the greenhouse. Dr Watson also happened to notice that Ripley had torn out all his orchids. Then there was the bag of quick lime under the bench, obviously to cover the smell, and the pruning saw lying on the potting bench." He lifted from the side table an ordinary-looking garden saw, of the type used for trimming fruit trees. "He never pruned an orchid with this!"

"But if Ripley buried the poor woman's extremities in the greenhouse, why dump her torso in the river?" Bradstreet asked.

"It is a simple matter of volume," Holmes said. "He had no more room in his pots."

"It is most extraordinary," Bradstreet said, "I don't care what you say, Mr Holmes." My friend shrugged and closed his eyes. "You must admit, Dr Watson, that bottle of ether was a close thing."

"Indeed it was," I said gravely.

Bradstreet rose, "It will take a least a day to air the rooms out. I've already sent one man to hospital from the fumes. We can hardly conduct a proper investigation until then." He walked to the door and opened it.

"I'm sure you'll do your best," Holmes muttered.

The inspector leaned close to me and whispered, "He'll be all right, then?"

I nodded and we shook hands. Bradstreet appeared considerably relieved.

"Well, goodbye, Mr Holmes. Dr Watson." He closed the door.

For several minutes, Holmes sat perfectly still in his armchair, eyes shuttered, fingers laced together on his chest. I almost thought he had dropped off to sleep, until he chuckled to himself. His thin lips twitched with a smile, and then he laughed.

"What is it?" I asked, laughing myself, for his laughter was quite contagious.

He opened his eyes. "Oh, nothing. Just a passing fancy."

"Go on then," I said. "Tell me. You cannot keep it to yourself."

He sat up, alert, with a mischievous twinkle in his eyes. "Well, I may have been confused by that blow to the head, or perhaps the ether fumes, but I would almost be prepared to swear before a coroner's inquest that Ripley's cat *intentionally* tripped him."

"Holmes!"

He smiled like the devil himself. "You see now why I detest cats, Watson. They are more intelligent than science would have us believe. Look at her sitting contentedly in your lap. There is a criminal mind behind those nefarious yellow eyes equal to the worst criminal in London." He lit a cigarette and slumped back into his chair. Mrs Ripley's cat yawned and closed her eyes.

Holmes watched her from beneath his own hooded lids. "She is happy now, because she has had her revenge." ❧

The author tells us, "I'm not very adventurous, unless you count my recent three-mile move to the state of Mississippi. And author resumés are so tedious, unless they're your resumé, in which case they're usually too short. I'm most proud of my family: my two boys and their wonderful, patient mother; but that's not likely to fill a quarter page. People say I should open a restaurant, but I like to cook, not work. I could write a homage to all the cats I've loved before, who've wandered in and out my door. There is always the temptation to pen something terribly clever about yourself, but after a time it no longer seems so clever as it once did and you usually end up regretting it. I'm hoping I will have a supernatural mystery novel to hawk by the time this story is published."

MRS RIPLEY'S CAT

ALPHONSE

by Sandra Beswetherick

"ALPHONSE," I called softly into the back yard. "Alphonse, are you out there?" I'd already searched the house, quietly tip-toeing throughout. The reason for my caution was Edward. He was currently searching my CD collection in the living room for something romantic we could listen to. "Alphonse?" I called one last time. Maybe, if luck was with me, he'd stay out all night.

I closed the door, turned back into the kitchen, and slipped the chicken casserole I'd prepared earlier in the day into the oven. I then arranged a few toast rounds spread with bruschetta, as appetizers, on a tray. This was the first time I'd invited Edward for dinner. Alphonse did not approve of men being invited to the house. In fact, I suspected him of having tried to kill one once. So I'd been keeping Alphonse a secret from Edward and their confrontation delayed.

I had met Edward in a food bank, of all places. Considerate, understanding, and so very patient, Edward was quite different from the men I'd been dating. He always seemed to have something pleasant to say to fellow volunteer and customer alike. "It's wonderful the way you treat everyone as if they were special," I'd shyly confided to him one morning when we were working together. Surprisingly he'd grasped my hand, looked deep into my eyes, and smiled. "You do know, Janet, that there is someone who's more than special to me."

Edward and I had been out together on several occasions to restaurants and to movies. At the time of my dinner invitation, my thinking was I could no longer postpone the inevitable. Right now, though, I've quite changed my mind. I was falling in love with Edward and didn't want him frightened off. As I poured two glasses of wine, I warily listened for sounds of Alphonse.

Not until I'd carried the wine to the living room, did I realize I didn't need to worry any longer about Alphonse's whereabouts.

Edward was kneeling on the carpet, intently sifting through my CDs. Opposite him, amber eyes blazing and plumed tail lashing in a fury, crouched Alphonse. I could almost read his thoughts as he studied his next victim. "Well now, who is it we have here this time?"

Edward looked up, then, as if he'd felt the intensity of Alphonse's gaze. "Hello, cat," he said. "I didn't hear you come in."

This was a much better beginning than Sidney's remark, which had been. "I see you have a cat." Even Alphonse heard the condescending tone in Sidney's voice, promptly turned his back, and stalked regally from the room. Just as I was beginning to wonder where he'd got to, I heard the rattling jingle of keys being batted down the hallway. Alphonse had found Sidney's keys on the hall table and was really giving them a go. Sidney jumped to his feet and snatched the keys away, barely avoiding a scratch. "Stupid cat," he'd said, glaring at Alphonse.

Alphonse had glared back as if he'd planned this all along. "Now that you have your keys, get lost."

"I'm Edward," Edward introduced himself, setting the CDs aside, and giving his full attention to the large, white cat silently studying him. Did it please Alphonse as much as me, I wondered, that Edward didn't find it silly addressing a cat? Edward then slowly and politely extended his hand. My breath caught as Alphonse narrowed his eyes and flattened his ears, perhaps recalling Robert's treatment.

I'd actually thought I'd stood a chance with Robert. Ruggedly handsome, outgoing, and athletic, he was captain of his football team. Robert had also thought he'd stood a chance with me. Otherwise he wouldn't have said, "I adore cats," with such assurance. But when Robert grabbed Alphonse, tossed him in the air as though he were a football, and vigorously rubbed Alphonse's fur once he'd caught him again, it was obvious he neither adored nor understood felines. Alphonse, looking more like an outraged dust mop than a cat, squirmed free of Robert's clutches and bolted from the room. Not until the end of the evening, when I retrieved Robert's expensive leather jacket from the coat rack, did I realize how vengeful Alphonse could be.

"WHAT'S your name, cat?" Edward asked, his hand still outstretched. Alphonse at last leaned forward as far as he could without tipping over and delicately sniffed.

"It's Alphonse," I answered from the doorway. "Rod, my late husband, named him."

"Ah," Edward said, and then turned to Alphonse again. "A noble name for a noble cat."

Did you hear that, Alphonse? I silently inquired. *A noble name, a noble cat.*

Martin had found Alphonse's name hilarious. "What a weird name to give a cat." Insulting both Alphonse and Rod, I felt. And Alphonse did not take well to derisive laughter. It was Martin who Alphonse had tried to kill. He clambered to the top of the high bookcase — how he managed it without sprouting wings I'll never know — and dislodged a heavy potted plant that sailed down, narrowly missing Martin's head.

After Martin, I'd given up on dating. Not that I considered Alphonse's reactions unreasonable, but because there seemed to be no one who suited us both. Alphonse had been Rod's cat, although following Rod's death, Alphonse and I had grown closer, sustaining each other through our grief. I would never abandon Alphonse, but I worried he wouldn't accept anyone in Rod's place.

"MY GRANDFATHER had a Manx cat he named Caesar," Edward said, resting back on his heels, accepting the glass of wine. "That cat wore the name well, imperious and proud; he lorded over everyone, including my granddad. Except the times I arrived for a visit. Then Caesar dropped that persona and snuck into the woods to play hide and seek with me." His smile expanded, and his eyes seem to dance at the memory. "Then, there was Sheba, Aunt Lily's cat. A queen of cats if there ever was one."

Do you hear that, Alphonse, I thought at him, *Edward must like cats.*

Alphonse sat, his ears pricked and focused on Edward, listening to his every word. When Edward and I went into the kitchen for dinner, Alphonse came with us and listened to our conversation there. He looked from one of us to the other as we spoke, watching our faces as well.

What was going on behind those inquisitive eyes, I wondered. What were his feline instincts telling him, and what conclusions was he drawing? That Edward was loving, kind, and honest or that he was mean, deceitful, and lying through his teeth.

Edward looked down at him approvingly. "You're a well-mannered cat, Alphonse, patiently waiting, not demanding attention or snacks while we eat." Alphonse surprised me when he answered in a short, sharp meow of agreement. That he chose to speak to Edward at all, I regarded as a good sign.

I LOST TRACK of Alphonse for a while, enjoying Edward's company, his conversation, his smile, the warmth of his eyes. Only after Edward gently kissed the palm of my hand, did I notice Alphonse was gone. Oh dear! I looked round the room and under the table.

"What's wrong?" Edward asked.

I tried to reassure him with a smile. "Nothing. Alphonse must have gone out for the night." I sincerely hoped he wasn't up to any mischief. It was after Martin had grabbed me by the arm and pulled me into a tight embrace that Alphonse had attempted homicide.

Had I tightly shut the door of the closet where Edward's coat now hung, I wondered. Where had Edward left his keys or anything else that belonged to him?

It was while I was making coffee, with Edward once again in the living room after helping with the clearing-up, that I heard the cat flap open, then close. I turned round and glimpsed the tail end of Alphonse bounding across the hallway. I hurriedly set the coffee aside. *Alphonse — what are you doing? Please don't ruin this for me. I thought you were starting to like Edward.*

Alphonse was sitting at Edward's feet. Edward was bending over. On the carpet between them lay the body of a mouse.

"Oh, Alphonse," I breathed. How many such gifts, tokens of his acceptance and affection, had he brought to lay at Rod's feet, and then mine.

I looked at Edward, my hand at my throat. Would he recognize Alphonse's generosity?

He was Edward, and I shouldn't have worried.

"Aren't you the good hunter, Alphonse!" Edward exclaimed. "Well done, old man!" When Alphonse looked down at that mouse, sorely tempted, Edward thanked him for the morsel and politely declined. "I'm much too full after Janet's lovely dinner, and I do think you'd enjoy it more." When Alphonse butted his head, then arched his back against Edward's proffered hand, I knew we three would be all right.   🐾

Sandra Beswetherick's short stories have appeared in magazines published in Australia, Great Britain, the USA, and Sweden. Her story "The Twilight Zone on the Rideau Canal" is part of the Canadian mystery anthology Locked Up *launched in April 2007. Sandra lives near Seeley's Bay, Ontario, with her husband and two cats. They share their property with deer, coyote, the odd skunk, and several raccoons.*

by Sandra Beswetherick

TREE

I think that I shall never pat
a tree as lovely as a cat
but gene engineering, given time,
will breed us trees much more feline.

Instead of bark, a silky fur
a tree with low and rumbling purr.
In the future, I will bet,
a tree will be the perfect pet.

A pussy willow to meow and beg
while tiger lilies rub your leg.
Dogwood trees won't howl at night
but bark the catwoods to a fright.

A tree will not have fleas or lice
although it also won't chase mice.
And one more thing makes trees much better:
a tree does not need kitty litter.

So one day soon, although not yet,
a tree will be the perfect pet.

— **Geoffrey A. Landis**

A SMALL SACRIFICE

by Michael Northrop

To SAY THAT Roger Saltonstal was up to no good would be selling him short: He was up to evil. Specifically, he was preparing to sacrifice the family cat to the Egyptian deity Set, god of evil, chaos, and infertility, and murderer of Osiris. Roger was something like 1/64th Egyptian and was what would generally be called troubled. He had accepted Set as his dark lord shortly after doing a report on Egyptian mythology in school the year before.

As rinky-dink, almost laughable, as this may seem — a sullen teen making dubious claims on his heritage and adopting an ancient god as a complement to his death-metal music — there were signs that he just might be on to something. As he scattered the beetle husks he'd meticulously collected over the course of the summer into the molten wax of a burning black candle, the house seemed alive with ancient energies, the forgotten gods perhaps stirred by the sudden attention. As he arranged freezer-burned, raw chicken parts around the improvised altar in his family's New Hampshire home, his nostrils pinched in and he inhaled arid desert air. He could practically taste the sand particles, and it thrilled him.

The house was empty, a responsibility that Roger, at age 17, was thought to be up to. His parents were at a cocktail party, a company function of some sort. He didn't ask, just greedily accepted the opportunity. His sister, who often protected the cat from his casual cruelty, was staying over at a friend's house. That left only Roger and Corporal Peck 'n Paw, a gray cat of indeterminate breed who was generally, and mercifully, referred to as The Corporal. Though pinned belly-up to the stained cherry-wood table by two short, elastic cords, the sort used to secure luggage to carts, The Corporal continued to squirm and, in recent moments, to eye the chicken parts.

It was edging toward nine o'clock, and the house was dark save for the lone candle in the living room. Reflected light caught The Corporal's sensitive eyes. It was, of course, the knife, the longest and cruelest the kitchen had to offer. The plan was to sacrifice the cat as an offering to Set and a blow against Bastet, the beloved cat-headed goddess of women, children, and fertility. A female cat would have been better, a female kitten best, but Roger was making do with what he had.

Benign Bastet, Goddess of the East, along with the destructive, lioness-headed Sekhmet, Goddess of the West, represented balance in nature. Thus the blood rite was also meant to unbalance things in a way that Roger was sure the God of Chaos, a being whose head was that of some unidentifiable animal, would appreciate. Both goddesses were represented and served by cats, but it was Bastet whom Roger sought to offend. He wanted no truck with Sekhmet, a malevolent entity whose name came from the ancient word *Sekhem,* meaning to be violent.

That was the plan, anyway — sacrifice The Corporal, toss the carcass in the woods out back, and plead ignorance when asked where the cat was — but when you worship a chaotic god you can't be too surprised when things go a bit off course. Roger brought the point of the knife close to the Corporal's head. He intended to torture the creature first, to inflict pain that would make Bastet herself cry out; and he meant to begin with a nice blinding. At first the cat watched the blade's approach with curiosity, his body continuing to squirm even as his head held still; but as the point neared the yellow orb of his right eye, The Corporal turned his head away almost demurely.

Roger reached down with his left hand and roughly turned the cat's head back around, then pressed it down hard against the tabletop. The Corporal hissed and jerked hard, freeing his right hind leg, which he immediately began kicking against the lower of the two elastic cords. Roger ignored this and focused on the delicate film of the eye's curved surface. An inch out, he steadied his hand and pushed the knife forward. Would it ooze? Bleed? Roger was hypnotized with anticipation.

Both hind legs free now, The Corporal thrust his lower body out and raked his claws into Roger's wrist with three quick kicks. Thin contrails of blood appeared on Roger's skin as he pulled his arm away. The Corporal contorted explosively, shrugging his head out from under the top cord. Roger slashed out with the knife but the cat was already scrambling off the table. Roger heard The Corporal land with a soft thump on the carpeting on the other side; and in the time it took Roger to run around his makeshift altar, the cat had made it to the foot of the stairs.

"Son of a . . ." said Roger. "Dammitdammitdammit!"

The Corporal tore up the stairs, taking them one and two at a time in straight, quick leaps with no arc to them, no wasted motion. Roger thudded up behind him, taking the steps by memory, the knife bobbing along in his right hand. Not the sporting type, he hadn't done anything especially athletic since a half-hearted attempt at skateboarding in junior high. He was winded by the landing and swore under his breath as he made the turn and took the final steps to the second floor. He moved into the darkened hallway and hit the light switch just in time to see a gray tail disappear into his sister's room.

The candle continued to burn down in the living room. A beetle carapace floating on the melted wax drifted up against the wick and began to issue a sickly sweet smoke.

Roger stood in the doorway of his sister's room.

"Game over," he said as he spotted a pair of glowing eyes. A few feet away, he figured, probably up on the dresser. He turned the knife in his hand, switching to the *Psycho* grip, the blade now pointed down toward the floor, but he stopped half a step into the room. The eyes were not close and small, they were large and farther away, up against the far wall, if he had to guess.

The ceremony was reaching its climax now. He had meant it all — the captive cat, the profane symbols, the bird flesh and bug husks — as an affront to Bastet, but Bastet was slow to anger. Not so, her Western sister. Jaws opened in the dark, and Roger knew he was in trouble. He knew, because house-cats didn't growl like that.

The Corporal hunkered down under the bed. His ears pricked up at the first sounds, but he crouched deep, ears back, when the screaming started. Finally, the noise subsided and the cat crept forward. The coppery smell of shed blood still hung in the air, but the cat was willing to chance a sprint to the hallway. The boy was gone — mostly — and there were chicken parts downstairs.   ❖

Michael Northrop is the author of Gentlemen, *a mystery for young adults and teens, published by Scholastic in April 2009. As a child, he once stepped on a yellow jacket hive and was quite puffy for days. His first pet was a gray cat named Ghost.*

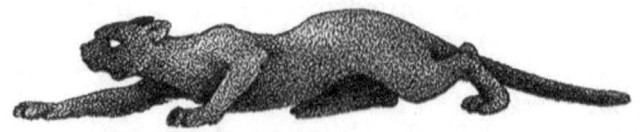

A SMALL SACRIFICE

MUEZZA'S GARDEN

by Paula R. Stiles

THERE WERE just as many liars back home as there had ever been in Baghdad. "I'm having trouble sleeping," Billy told the doctor at the VA. "Is that normal? Am I okay?"

The doc assured him that he was fine, then made out a prescription for sleeping pills. He didn't even look Billy in the eye.

" 'Army strong,' my ass," Billy muttered to himself as he left the building. He got the prescription filled, trying not to think too hard about how swallowing the whole bottle on top of the previous prescription would be a pretty quick exit, quicker than some he'd seen.

Every day, when he took the bus home from work, he got off and limped past a sign pasted on a telephone pole. It was one of those sad, pathetic posters declaring that the owner had lost a kitten. It gave a phone number for anyone who might see said kitten. The poster had faded. It made him sad, yet he couldn't . . . quite . . . look away. The black-and-white photo of the black-and-white kitten made him want to find the creature, named "Missy," even though he knew she must be dead by now, lost for sure. He understood about being lost.

The night he got off the bus and heard the mew, it stopped him dead. He'd just been to the grocery store, later in the evening to avoid the crowds. Crowds made him itchy and nervous. Grocery stores in general made him itchy and nervous: too cold, too many people, too many aisles hiding things from him, far too much choice. He hated them. And yet, living alone, cut loose from the Army after his medical discharge, he had to go out and take care of business. He couldn't sit at home, curl up in a ball and bite his knees. That just wasn't an option.

Would a simple "Welcome home, Billy" have killed anybody to say?

He heard the kitten's cry over the sound of the bus. At first, he couldn't locate her. But as he looked around, he noticed a little black-and-white figure, surrounded by a nimbus of light from the streetlamp, sitting and grooming.

As soon as he turned toward her, the kitten ran up to him. She looked *exactly* like the kitten in the photo. He blinked and then, slowly and painfully, levered himself down to pet her.

"Hey, sweety," he said uncertainly.

The kitten sniffed at his outstretched hand, then moved up against his fingers. He'd had many cats growing up, and dogs, and horses. He remembered the horses wistfully. He didn't think his leg would take riding anymore. He'd given up a lot of things after being pinned under a Humvee one hot morning in a small village outside Baghdad.

As he scratched the kitten's ears, she purred. Animals had always liked him.

THE GUYS in his unit had laughed at his fondness for feeding the local strays. They'd laughed a lot less when a few old men waved to them and called, *"Salaam aleikum!"* the next time they went out on patrol.

"Why'd they do that?" Joe Rikers asked as they drove by, the hot dust curling up in a whirlwind like a Disney djinn behind them. Already, the morning cool was burning off into desert fire. Joe looked right at Billy.

Billy shrugged. "You're asking me?"

Joe shrugged back. "Hey, you're the Arabic interpreter."

This was true. Billy had demonstrated an aptitude for languages in basic training and a willingness to take the intensive Arabic course. A year later, there he was in Iraq, doing the go-back-and-forth with the locals.

Billy thought hard about Joe's question, but couldn't come up with anything. "Dunno. Must've done something they liked."

He had his answer a few days later when he was feeding one of the strays in a late-afternoon shadow on the street. One of the old men approached him, leaning on a cane. Billy had learned already to be wary of Iraqis approaching him for any reason. Yes, some were friendly. Others, the ones who slapped you on the back and swore they were your best friends, would become, as soon as your back was turned, your bitterest enemies, even insurgents. They laid mines for you on the road. They swarmed out like hornets, muffled in scarves to hide their identities so that they could attack and then come back for more Coke and candy bars the next day.

But this old man in his long, white dress and head covering had shown no such previous false heartiness and seemed genuinely frail. So, Billy engaged in an awkward conversation in Arabic about the weather while the cats scampered around them, bold and timid in equal measure. They darted forward to grab the slices of meat Billy had smuggled out to them from the mess hall. One old girl with tortoise-shell striations even came up to him and nibbled his fingers. The old man smiled in what looked like benevolent amusement at the cats' interest in Billy.

At the end of the conversation, Billy admitted that he had to go back to the barracks. The old man waved his hand vaguely over him in a sort of blessing. "Allah loves the man who is kind to cats."

"Oh?" Billy said. "I'd never heard that."

The old man nodded. "The Prophet, blessings be upon him, had a cat." He smiled, a broad expression that revealed teeth of many colors. Yet the cheerfulness in it made Billy feel guilty and impressed at the same time. Guilty that he could not make this man's life better. Impressed that this old man could still find such simple joy in a conversation about a cat in the middle of a war.

Then, the first evening call to prayer went out and the old man hurried away. As he did, Billy thought he saw a woman standing down the street, half-hidden around the corner. She appeared to be dressed all in black in the evening light. Even her face was covered, not an unusual occurrence here.

Billy heard the old man call out to him a cheery *"Maasalaama"* and waved back. When he turned again toward the woman, she had vanished.

HE DECIDED he'd better do some research to figure out what was going on. Maybe the locals were being nice to him because he liked cats and maybe they were just shining him on. The latter option was always there, whether he liked it or not.

What he found made him even more curious. "Did you know that the Prophet Muhammad had a cat?" he told Joe later, back at the barracks while he was looking up the information. "Her name was Muezza." He kept reading. "Actually . . . it says here she was his *favorite* cat, so I guess he had more than one."

"Yeah, yeah," Joe said. "You gonna get off soon? I gotta e-mail my wife."

"What? Yeah, sure, okay. Gimme a minute. Yeah, it says here, Muhammad found a cat sleeping on the sleeve of his robe once and cut off the sleeve instead of disturbing the cat. Goofy. And it says here the ancient Egyptians really had a thing for cats, says there was this cat-headed goddess called 'Bastet'." He chuckled, then sobered as he saw Joe tapping his fingers impatiently on the table. "Yeah, okay, I'm getting off."

He was still thinking it over in his bunk after lights out. Was that why the old man had been nice to him? Could it be as simple as being nice to a cat?

AND NOW here he was in the street, scratching the ears of a little stray who might be called "Missy."

"Sweetie, you need a home," he said. "You got a

home?" The kitten mewed. She looked too thin and a little mangy, as if she hadn't had a good meal in a week. He picked her up. "Okay, let's take you home and give you something to eat, see later if maybe you've got someone missing you somewhere."

As he carried the kitten toward his apartment, he thought he tasted sand. A hot wind seemed to slide down the road. He fought down the shiver and told himself it was just a flashback. He wasn't too sure when he'd become casual enough about flashbacks to call the occurrence of one "just," but he was there now. The shrink he'd talked to, all too briefly in the hospital after his injury, had told him that he would feel dislocated for a while, but that it would pass. Nobody had told him that all he had to do was close his eyes on a hot summer's day and be back in Iraq. Or that he'd shiver all summer long because even a hot summer down south wasn't as hot as the Middle East. Nobody had told him a lot of things he might have found useful. The Army's requiem for his career, aside from his small pension, had been remarkably short.

IN IRAQ, the day everything changed, the old man had tried to give him a cat, a little thing, black and white. "It is wrong to trade a cat for money or goods," the old man said, trying to push the cat into Billy's arms. "A cat should be a gift, cherished."

"I'm sorry, but I can't take her," Billy said, honest regret in his voice. "The Army won't let me."

The old man looked sad, but didn't push it. "Perhaps Allah will give you one someday. I believe there is a special garden for those who treat cats well, a special heaven for them when they feel weary in spirit. Perhaps you will find that someday."

"Yeah . . . well, thanks." Billy was puzzled by the old man's words. *A garden?* What the hell did that mean?

But Joe was calling him and they had to be down the road by noon. So he waved to the old man and got in the patrol vehicle and off they went.

They didn't get fifty yards before a front tire blew. Billy never did find out what had happened. It felt like a grenade, or a mine in the street. All he knew was that one minute, Joe was driving and he was riding shotgun and the next the world jumbled. The Humvee windshield came up at him like the withers of a bucking horse. Then there was an enormous impact. His leg started to go numb.

He came to, lying in the street, with the Humvee on top of him. Above him, cirrus clouds formed cuneiform symbols on an Egyptian tomb. Somewhere, far, far away, he knew he was in shock. When he tried to move, nothing would work.

He sensed movement coming out of the dusty, mud brick houses — insurgents, muffled and carrying guns. He didn't feel a thing, not even regret or fear. He wondered with a vague sadness if Joe had gotten out, even though he couldn't hear Joe at all. He was going to die. That he knew.

A cat scampered past his nose, bringing a whiff of jasmine and cool palms. Then another. Down the street past the insurgents, Billy thought he saw the old woman in black again. The insurgents, instead of coming closer, hesitated.

A wave of people came out of the houses — young, old, men and women and children. They flooded into the street and around the patrol vehicle. The insurgents were not only lost in the crowd, they were swept away as if they were nothing. Suddenly, he could hear again. Joe was yelling his name from the other side of the Humvee. Joe was all right.

"Thank God," Billy whispered, not sure what he was thankful for.

The old man who had given him the cat knelt down creakily beside him and laid a hand on his head. "Do not worry," he whispered in Arabic. "Everything is all right now."

Billy closed his eyes. He heard water running in a nearby fountain, smelled jasmine and tasted fresh dates, heard the pitter-patter of cat feet, little cat cries.

THEN HE WOKE in the hospital and discovered that while they had been able to save his leg, they hadn't been able to save his career.

Now, back home, as he limped down the street, he could almost smell jasmine again. It must have been a trick of the wind, or his mind. Maybe one of his neighbors had some similar flower in their garden, even though it was heading into fall with no Indian Summer to cushion the blow. He shivered, cursing his addiction to the desert heat one more time.

As he passed a hedge, the kitten leaped out of his arms. Startled, he let out a "Hey!" of protest. Even as he stumbled after her, she scampered down the sidewalk and abruptly swerved into the hedge.

He should have let her go, but he couldn't. He liked that kitten. Limping after her, he came to an opening in the hedge. He peered through it into the darkness. Inside, he heard running water and smelled jasmine.

He stepped inside.

Now he could see somewhat better. Starlight that the street lamps had blotted out shone into the garden as his eyes adjusted to the dim light. Ahead of him, the kitten scampered across the garden toward a dark figure standing in shadow.

"Who's there?" he called out, his heart beating fast. He wanted to be afraid, but something about the garden converted the fear into something else, something he couldn't name. "Who are you?"

The figure stepped forward. She was dressed in black like the old woman he had seen before his accident. He let out a breath that seemed loud in the garden, as if he had been holding it in since Iraq, a hot, desert wind. As he did, some of his pain flowed away.

The figure in front of him changed, lightened, as she stepped forward. She looked up at him. For a second, he saw cat's eyes. Then, she was just a young woman dressed in the linen, shoulderless dress he had seen in pictures of Ancient Egypt. Dark hair in countless braids hung down on either side of her lovely dark face.

"Who are you?" he asked.

"You know me," she answered.

"Yes," he admitted. "But . . ." He trailed off, embarrassed by an ignorance that should not have been his fault.

She smiled at him, not showing her teeth as if she knew it would make her look threatening. "My name is Bastet." The kitten leaped into her arms. "This is Muezza."

" 'Missy'," he said, making the connection. "She was the lost cat."

Bastet nodded. "She was lost and then you found her for me. I knew you would. I find all of the ones that belong to me, no matter how lost they are." Small bells tinkled in the darkness when she tilted her head. "As I found you."

He turned, taking in the fountain, the walls covered with greenery, the date palms, the soft grass. Underneath it, he sensed sand. "What is this place? Where is it?"

"My garden, of course. And Muezza's."

He turned back to her, wondering where the pain in his leg, gnawing at him for months, had gone. "I don't understand. Why am I here? Why me?"

Bastet came forward and pushed the kitten gently into his arms. This time, he took her. The kitten purred softly, as soothing as waves on the beach.

"We came to welcome you home, Billy."   🐾

The author tells us she is a forty-one-year-old American who has sold science-fiction, fantasy, and horror stories to Strange Horizons, Writers of the Future, Arkham Tales, *and many other markets. This story was inspired by too many* MISSING *posters on telephone poles and by the author's experiences. Medically separated from the Peace Corps after two years in a West African Muslim village, she recently noticed similar stories from injured Iraq War veterans. She wrote this story for them.*

THE CLOWDER

by Orrin Grey

THE OLD LADY across the hall had, like, fifty or sixty cats. She had them all named: Rufus and Chester, Theodore and Elizabeth. On the rare occasion that you encountered her out in the hall or in the elevator, she would regale you with stories about them. So-and-so had a hurt paw, or such-and-such had knocked over a glass that morning.

Her apartment was the same size as ours, which is to say not very large, and yet I never heard the cats or smelled them, not even on her when she came outside. I used to believe her, that she had the cats; and their mysterious scarcity perplexed me as a child, until I asked my mom.

"That crazy old bat?" Mom asked. "Oh, she's sweet, don't get me wrong, but she hasn't owned a cat since the day she moved in here. Building's got a policy against them."

I knew that last part, actually. It's why I wasn't allowed to own a kitten. The reason for my asking had in truth been more than curiosity. It was going to lead into a request for a cat of my own. "After all," I had intended to say, "if she can have fifty or sixty cats, there's no reason at all that I can't have just one, right?"

But she didn't have fifty or sixty cats. She had the

same number of cats as me: none. She was just a little crazier than I was, and had somehow convinced herself, that she was surrounded by feline companions. All three of her children, one son and two daughters, were dead. As was her husband. I had no doubt that she had owned a great many cats once, maybe even as many as fifty or sixty, back when she still lived in a house somewhere. But now she owned none. At least, no real ones.

She still had her imaginary ones, and they kept her plenty busy. I had been asked into her apartment only once, when my mom sent me over to beg for some shortening. Inside, the old lady was constantly petting invisible animals, lifting them up and moving them out of the way, stepping carefully so as to avoid hypothetical paws and tails. She had several massive bags of cat food that she kept in trash cans in the kitchen. Whenever she opened her door, she always blocked the doorway with her feet to prevent her phantom charges from getting out.

"I do let them out on the fire escape sometimes," she confided in me one day in the elevator. I was getting home from school, and she was getting home from the grocer's down the street. I was carrying her bags.

I always made it a point to be extra nice to her after I learned that she didn't have a real cat either. Most people were kind enough to her, but few had the patience to listen to her delusions. I was one of the few.

And sometimes, though only at night and only alone in my room, I tried to pretend that *I* had an imaginary kitten. I would be sprawled on my bed watching TV or trying to do algebra homework, chewing the eraser off my mechanical pencil, and I would reach out and pet the air next to me, as though a kitten were curled up on the comforter purring away. Sometimes it did make me feel better, but usually it just made me feel lonely.

ONE DAY the old lady across the hall had to go to the hospital. I don't know why. It wasn't an emergency or anything, because she knew that she was going in advance. She was only going to be there a few days, she said, and could I please check in on her cats while she was gone?

She left me a spare key to her apartment and strict instructions on the feeding of the cats, how much and how often, as well as a notation that Sidney was the runt of the bunch and that I was to make sure that she got enough to eat, even if I had to feed her separately from the others.

I took the key and put it on the key ring where I kept the only other two keys I had, one to the door downstairs and one to our apartment. I was sixteen, but my mom didn't trust me to drive in the city yet. Besides, there wasn't anywhere I really needed to go that I couldn't easily walk or take the bus. I promised to keep an eye on the old lady's cats, and she fished into her purse and gave me a crumpled five-dollar bill.

We hadn't really agreed on any payment, and I would have tried to give the money back, but she just winked at me and shuffled off.

ORIGINALLY I planned to do nothing, of course. It's not like the old lady could ever possibly know what I did or didn't do while she was gone. The cats wouldn't go hungry or die or anything. They weren't even real. And I would feel enormously silly walking around an empty apartment and pouring cat food and milk into bowls.

But then I started to feel guilty. I *had* promised to do what she asked. And it didn't really matter that there weren't any real cats, I could still putter around her apartment, keep an eye on things, and go through the motions because I had promised her that I would. For some reason I didn't want to break a promise to the crazy old lady.

And the five in my pocket didn't help. I felt bad enough taking her money; I didn't need taking her money *and* not doing the job on my conscience.

So I wound up spending Friday night in her apartment. Everything in the place was decorated in a really old style, like my grandma's house before she died. One of those couches with tall wooden legs stood in the living room in front of an old TV, and there was a bronze birdcage in one corner. I wondered if it maybe held imaginary birds, but she hadn't given me any instructions regarding their care, so I didn't worry about it.

I sat my backpack down next to one of the couch's legs. I figured if I was going to be spending pointless time in an empty apartment at least I could get some homework done. First, though, I made the rounds, looking in every room, making sure nothing was amiss. Naturally, nothing was.

I sat down on the couch and took out a chemistry book, held it in my lap, and tried to concentrate on working some of the homework problems. But I couldn't. I kept thinking about the damned imaginary cats I was supposed to be taking care of.

Finally, after what was probably not more than five minutes of attempted studying, I put the book aside and walked into the kitchen. I opened up one of the big trash cans, trying to imagine dozens of cats scurrying forward, getting underfoot, purring in anticipation. I poured the food into all the indicated bowls, and then I went to the refrigerator and got one of the four jugs of milk that sat inside, unscrewed the lid, and poured some into a large metal bowl near the others.

Lastly, I picked up two smaller bowls, filled one with food and one with milk, and then walked out of the kitchen.

"Sidney," I cooed quietly, feeling self-conscious even though I was totally alone. "Come on, girl." I fed Sidney in the bathroom, so that she would make sure and get plenty of food and not get butted out by the other cats.

Then, feeling better, I went and sat back down on the couch. I turned on the TV and turned the volume low. It was black and white and only had an old rabbit-ear antenna, so it didn't get more than a couple of channels, but I didn't care because I just wanted it as a background to my studying anyway. I looked back down at the chemistry homework held in my lap.

AND I MUST HAVE dozed off, because the next

thing I heard was a window being opened. I snapped awake. My chemistry book had slipped from my lap and was lying, open to the wrong page, on the couch beside me. It was 11:45. The TV was still on, as was the lamp I had been using to read by, but the TV was displaying static. I had turned the volume down so low that I could barely hear it, just a distant and indistinct buzzing, like the sound of far-off traffic.

But I wasn't listening for the static, though. My ears were straining to a different sound, the companion to the **shhunk** of the window opening. The sound of someone breaking into the old lady's apartment.

The window in question was in the bedroom, no doubt about it, through an open door to my right. I wasn't angled so that I could see the window, but I could hear whoever was coming in drag their way inside. Then the carpet swallowed their footsteps, but I knew that they were in the apartment with me. Even my heartbeat was louder than the TV static.

They must know that someone's here, my desperate mind supplied. *The light's on and so is the TV.*

Yes, I reminded myself, *but they probably think it's the old lady. The defenseless, senile old lady who has no family to miss her.*

And instead they had gotten the defenseless young girl, with only a single mother to miss her. I looked around for something to use as a weapon, or someplace to hide, but I came up with nothing better than my mechanical pencil with the chewed-up eraser. Before I could even take up that undoubtedly substandard weapon, however, the burglar came around the corner from the bedroom.

It was a young guy, probably not more than five or ten years older than me. He was dressed all in black, had short blonde hair, and wasn't wearing a mask. That bothered me, because in movies people who were committing crimes always wore masks unless they didn't plan on leaving witnesses.

"Well," he said, when he saw me. "I was expecting an old hag. This is much better."

I could have screamed, but he was holding a knife, long and silver in the light from the reading lamp. No one who heard me in the other apartments would get to me in time.

I just sat there on the couch, paralyzed. I could tell a lot from the tone of his voice. He was there to rob the place; he had planned to murder the old woman to do it. But since I was there instead, he had other plans for me first.

"You her granddaughter?" he asked, circling around the couch while I simply sat and stared. I tried to answer his question, but all I did was whimper.

"Oh," he said, in response to the tiny sound, "this is going to be fun."

But it wasn't fun, not for me and not for him, because all of a sudden there was a new sound. Like the television static, only infinitely louder. A hiss that rose up from every surface and every shadow to fill the room, like the sound of wind rushing through cattails, or steam escaping from a pipe. The man stopped, his knife poised out in front of him as though he were trying to use it to feel his way. For a moment he looked off balance, and then he stumbled back, away from me.

At first I didn't know what was going on, and then I heard another sound. A sound almost like fingernails on a chalkboard. A sound that only one thing in the world makes: an angry cat that is about to attack.

The would-be robber stumbled back again and the first red welts appeared across his cheek. I could see them then, indistinctly, like outlines in swirling smoke, or the clouds you point out when you're lying on your back in the park and you say, "That one looks like a cat."

It was as if the dust in the apartment congealed for a moment and there they were, dozens of them, fifty or sixty, crawling all over him, tearing at him with claws and teeth. He flailed, lashed out with his knife, but he still couldn't see them. He gutted air. Under the weight of the unseen cats, he fell back, struck a wall. A couple of them toppled from him, and were replaced by more. Perched on his face, tearing at his eyes and nose, was a tiny black and white cat, smaller than all the others. I knew that it was Sidney.

From the wall he stumbled forward again, missing the couch, careening across the living room. He was blind. It was almost as if the cats were steering him.

And maybe they were, for when he struck the window they all leapt free as one and he went out through the glass and then head over heels into the night. I heard the tinkling of the glass, but I didn't hear the wet Christmas tree thump when he struck the pavement below. The fire escape was outside the window of the master bedroom, not the living room, in this apartment.

I NEVER SAW or heard the cats again after that night. The police took my statement and figured that I accidentally knocked the robber out of the window during a scuffle. I told them I didn't know what had happened. It was the truth.

I was even nicer to the old lady after she came home from the hospital and never shook my head or rolled my eyes behind her back when she told some story about her innumerable cats. And sometimes, whenever I was feeling particularly lonely, I would swear that, even though I was in my own room in my own apartment and the door was shut, I could feel something warm and soft press against me, or I would catch a flash of something tiny and black and white, moving, just out of the corner of my eye.   🐾

By the way, "clowder" is the collective noun for cats. "Kindle" is the collective for kittens — provided they are not of the same litter.

Orrin Grey lives in Kansas with his wife Grace and his two cats, Abracadabra and Feralina. His stories have appeared in several magazines and anthologies, including Thirteen Stories, Maelstrom, The Willows, *and* Bound for Evil. *Orrin.grey@gmail.com is his e-mail. He doesn't generally write about himself in the third person, but occasional exceptions are made.*

THE SCRIBE VANISHES

by T. Lee Harris

I AWOKE to a woman screaming. This was, however, not unusual. Since I came to live in Pi-Ramesses, I'd shared a room with my cousin Ahmose over his widowed mother's linen shop. Aunt Tiaa was my mother's sister, and that side of the family was never noted for placidity. She was in rare form and the apprentices were taking the brunt of it.

At a fresh volley, Mose and I exchanged glances. We dressed fast and ran for it. I was luckier than Mose. He worked in the shop. I'd recently landed a job in the House of Life archives at the temple of Bastet.

The temple precincts were busier than usual with everyone preparing for the big festival that was coming up. Few pharoahs had seen the thirty-year reign required to hold their first Heb-Sed. The divine Ramesses II was celebrating his second. Ten days of feasting and fun. I was looking forward to it.

As I reached the Avenue of the Sphinxes leading to the temple gates, the wind shifted bringing the scent of roasting meat with it. It was probably Nakht's heavenly honey-roasted goose. Unfortunately, it also reminded me I'd left home without breakfast. The merchant stalls with their promise of food suddenly looked very inviting.

Up ahead, the High Priest's ancient servant, Huya,

hobbled out of the private quarters. He saw me, waved, and picked up his pace. This was impressive given both his age and the fact he'd nearly died from a blow to the head a short time ago. Forgetting the good smells, I hurried to meet him halfway.

It wound up being more than halfway, and the old man wheezed alarmingly. Leaning heavily on his stick, he glanced at the vicinity of my feet and flinched. "Ah, I see the Sacred One is with you."

By "Sacred One," he meant my companion, Nefer-Djenou-Bastet, and he said it much the same way he would say "Maddened Cobra That Spits Boiling Acid." I couldn't blame him. Neffi had only been with me for a short time; and, by and large, I agreed with Huya's opinion. Neffi is — or was — a temple cat, sacred to both the goddess Bastet and the Great God, Amun; and one day not so very long before, he decided he liked me. To say it changed my life is an understatement.

The old man eyed the cat. Neffi blinked and yawned, then fell to washing his hind leg. Satisfied that no nips, scratches, or unexpected wet noses were forthcoming, Huya said, "I'm glad I met you, Scribe. My master instructed me to leave a message in the House of Life that he wished to speak with you in private as soon as possible. Now I can take you to him myself."

For most junior scribes, being summoned by a High Priest was heady stuff. For me, it probably meant trouble. I wasn't expecting a tongue-lashing or anything like that. High Priest Pedibastet liked me and, because of my bond with Neffi, trusted me completely. As a result, his brother-in-law liked and trusted me, too. His brother-in-law was Crown Prince Merenptah, heir to the throne of the Two Lands. Somehow, I'd even managed to foil a plot against the Royal house. Trouble was, no one believed it had more to do with dumb luck and Neffi's uncanny sense for trouble than skill. Huya's manner warned me this was more of the same. And here I'd been planning on a nice, peaceful festival.

I glared at Neffi who was bathing his butt on the

walkway. "Let's go. This is probably your fault, anyway."

Pᴇᴅɪʙᴀsᴛᴇᴛ was reading in a splash of light from the garden portico. The remains of breakfast sat on a small folding table nearby. He greeted me, then greeted Neffi with a piece of bread from his breakfast plate. Neffi took the crust and leapt into the High-Priest's chair — right onto a tasseled silk cushion. I cringed. That cushion was probably the rarest and most expensive thing in the room. It was also Neffi's favorite place to sit. Now he was dropping pieces of half-chewed bread all over it.

Pedibastet chuckled and scratched the cat, who arched his back higher for more. "You're early. I didn't expect to see you for another hour."

Pedibastet scooped Neffi up, shook off the cushion and sat, plopping the big cat onto his lap as if he were a tiny kitten. Neffi's behavior with the Sem-Priest always amazed me. Now he lolled in the man's lap, front legs hanging down either side of the priest's knees, eyes closed, huge paws kneading the air in time to loud purrs. The old man fixed me with his formidable stare. "Are you ready for the festival?"

"Oh, yes, Sir! I've seen several of the three-year festivals since I came to stay in the capital. They were pretty memorable." I reflected with chagrin that some had been more memorable than others. Some post-festival mornings had been even *more* memorable, but I didn't bother the Sem-Priest with that.

"You're far too young to remember the Pharoah's first Heb-Sed, but it was a celebration like none before it. He performed all the physical feats himself in those days. The feasting and dancing went on day and night. The plans for this second look grander than the first."

"Will Prince Merenptah be standing in for the Pharoah again?"

"Of course." Pedibastet shook his head. "You've seen him, Sitehuti. There's little of the great Ramesses left these days. He can hardly walk across his audience chamber let alone run around the Heb-Sed enclosure.

A pity. You should have seen him in his prime. . . ." He trailed off, looking beyond me into the past, deep-set eyes seeing something I could only guess at. Abruptly, he refocused on me. "Preparations for the Census of the Cattle begin tomorrow."

I perked up. Any scribe would. We played an important part in accounting the wealth of the Two Lands that began the official Heb-Sed. "I heard a rumor that my old master is to be in charge of the Census."

"The rumor is correct. Khenemetamun-pa-sheri may be an arrogant prig, but he's still one of the best scribes in the city. You were fortunate to have studied under him. He leaves today for the Royal storehouses of Saqqara." He scratched Neffi under the chin. "You will be going with him."

There it was. "I'm going to be a scribe for the Census?"

"Yes and no. You're going with the scribal party for the Census, but your job is a little different. This is quite a puzzle, my boy."

"I'm not very good at puzzles, Your Eminence."

Pedibastet coughed his odd laugh. "You are too modest. If not for your ability with puzzles, there would be no great house of Ramesses today." Neffi hopped down, stretched, and sauntered off. I tried to keep an eye on him and pay attention to the Sem-Priest at the same time.

"It has come to the Royal Overseer's attention through anonymous letters that valuable items are disappearing from a particular storehouse."

"This is the storehouse where the Census is to take place?"

Neffi rooted for crumbs around the folding table.

"It is. Doubtless, the thievery has been going on for a while, but when items for the Heb-Sed vanish . . . this is not so easy to hide."

A spotted paw snaked up and fished around for more scraps from the breakfast remains. The table rocked dangerously. I sidled over and edged him away with my foot. "A thief would have to be very brazen or very foolish to think that would go unnoticed. There's more to this, isn't there, Sir?"

"Perceptive as usual, my young friend. The overseer of the storehouse is Ramesses' grandson, Heqamaatre."

It was almost as bad as I feared. The news left me holding my breath for a few heartbeats. Neffi took advantage of the pause to snatch a chunk of bread sopped in sesame paste and run for the gardens. "Ummmm . . . then I'll be conferring with him when I arrive."

"No. This investigation is being run from the palace. No need to mention this to Heqamaatre."

It *was* as bad as I feared. Pedibastet was avoiding telling me outright that the Pharoah's grandson was under suspicion.

Shouting erupted from the garden. I ignored it.

"Don't look so wary. The prince only wants you to accompany your teacher as his assistant. Look around. Ask questions. Notice things. It was fortunate he was appointed Scribe for the Census of the Cattle. No one will think twice about a former student assisting him."

"Yes, Your Eminence. Pardon me for mentioning this, but the Census takes several days. I'll need to pack. . . ."

The High-Priest cough-laughed again. "A chest containing all you'll need has already been requested from the temple stores. It will likely arrive at the school before you do."

"What if he leaves without me?"

"He's waiting for final instructions from the palace." The Sem-Priest sealed and handed me the scroll he'd been reading. "And here they are."

I DID NOT RACE to my appointment on wingéd feet. I may have been fortunate to study under Khenemeta-mun-pa-sheri, but I had counted myself doubly lucky to be out from under his thumb. Now I was right back there. Temporary or not, it wasn't a happy circumstance.

Outside, that aroma grabbed me again. It was sure to be a long day and no way did I want to face my old teacher on an empty stomach. Following my nose led me straight to Nakht's stall. Maybe I did have a little detecting skill after all.

I took my breakfast over to one of the low benches beside the shop. Ignoring the insistent rubbing at my knees, I took a bite and chewed appreciatively. It was mostly bread, but the succulent sauce had run all over it.

Someone poked me from behind and boomed, "Hurry up, kid, you're going to be late!"

The bite went down the wrong way. I was pounded on the back until the chunk of bread flew out. I whirled and found myself nose to scaled breastplate of the captain of Merenptah's Medjay guard. "Hey! Don't die with your mouth full, scribe. You can't recite the proper spells, that way."

I wiped my face. "Very funny, Djedmose. Let me guess. You've been sent to make sure I get where I'm going."

The Nubian's face split in a wicked grin. "Of course not. I'm leading the official guard for the scribal party. Just decided this morning. Finding you dawdling was a bonus."

I turned back to the table. My breakfast was gone and Neffi sat in its place, cleaning his face.

"Well, come on, then, no use hanging around here all morning." I snatched up the purring thief and slung him onto my shoulders. He complained — or maybe burped. I stomped off.

Chuckling, Djedmose caught up with me. It wasn't hard since his legs were a lot longer. "Don't get your loincloth in a knot, Scribe; I have good news. Our Anonymous isn't anymore. He's a mid-level scribe name of Sahathor. At the moment he isn't hot to point fingers, but I figure we can lean on him a little and who knows . . . ?" Djedmose's grin widened. "Looks like we're going to be busy."

I groaned.

WHEN we got to the school, preparations were well underway for the trip to Saqqara. Scribes, servants, and the escort contingent clogged the courtyard and spilled out into the street. My old master was in the main room, barking orders at scurrying students. Made me feel right at home. It took major effort to squash the urge to duck and run. I called to him over the hubbub. Khenemetamun-pa-sheri paled. I think he would have liked to slam the door in our faces and ram the bolt home. It wasn't Djedmose or me, but Neffi, who was still riding on my shoulders. Neffi and my former teacher had a long-standing animosity. Point of fact, this was the whole reason I was where I was. If he hadn't been so set on avoiding the cat, I wouldn't have been sent to the temple to take dictation from the High-Priest in his place. Come to think of it, I owed my old teacher a lot. Not all of it good.

Djedmose gave me a wink and took control of the aimlessly milling guard, shouting them into sharp order. It only took a glimpse of Merenptah's official seal on the scroll I held to convince Khenemetamun-pa-sheri to follow me into his study. There, behind closed doors, I handed over the letter. Neffi jumped off my shoulder to explore. My teacher's face was a road map of his progress through the message as he went from thinking I was simply a messenger to realizing I was included in his personal party. He glared at me over the edge of the papyrus. "So you've become a Royal spy."

"That's kind of an insulting description, Sir. I'd also like to point out that I didn't ask for this, either. It was the Crown Prince's idea and if you'd like to argue with him, I'll hold your writing kit."

He ground his teeth. "And that . . . that . . . cat demon!" It was a non-sequitur, but I couldn't fault him on that particular description, so I kept my mouth shut.

"I suppose this is why I was chosen to head the Census?"

I was aghast. "No, sir! Pedibastet himself told me you were chosen because you were the best scribe in the capital!"

"He said that?"

"Absolutely, Sir. Just this morning when he gave me the orders." Okay, not precisely his words, but close enough.

Mollified, he placed the letter in a bowl, poured water over it and moved it from side to side until all trace of ink was gone. "It's best this isn't read by anyone else." Suddenly, he jumped and yelped. "What's he doing over there?"

I turned and saw Neffi burrowed under a stack of papyri. He stood up, scattering scrolls and pranced over proudly holding a large beetle in his teeth. I reached for him, but he danced away. With a few crunches, his prize was gone.

My teacher's normally ruddy face took on a greenish tinge. He motioned abruptly toward the scattered scrolls, then fled the room. I shrugged and did as any good assistant would do: restacked the scrolls.

THE JOURNEY to Saqqara was mercifully uneventful. Neffi, who for some odd, un-catlike reason was calmed by riding on a boat, slept in the sun most of the way. No one was more relieved at this than my master. He spent the journey making the most of having an assistant by getting in as much dictation as possible. I must have caught up his correspondence until sometime into the next year.

When our entourage disembarked at the storehouse docks, Heqamaatre and his assistant met us. The overseer had inherited the Ramessid features, but on him they looked pinched rather than commanding. That might have had something to do with the fact he was anything but happy to see us.

After the preliminary greeting to the Master Scribe, the overseer pointed past my teacher toward Captain Djedmose. "That man is the captain of my uncle's personal guard. Why do you need a Royal Medjay contingent?"

The Master Scribe smiled. "Prince Merenptah honors me by lending his elite escort to my entourage. He wishes to ensure that his father's festival and the Census go smoothly." He swept a hand toward me. "Allow me to introduce my assistant, Sitehuti of Western Thebes."

Heqamaatre regarded me down the regal length of his nose, then blinked as Neffi yawned, leapt off the boat and strolled over to sit at my feet. "That's a temple cat."

I bowed. "Yes, Excellency. I'm afraid he's taken a liking to me."

"I see." Heqamaatre nodded warily. Neffi's reputation had a bad habit of preceding him.

As ASSISTANT to the official Census scribe, it fell to me to work with Heqamaatre's own assistant, Patwere, to ready our quarters. Patwere was a wiry man, just a little taller than me; and he was a chatterer.

I folded the Master Scribe's best cloak across the high bed and looked around. "Nice place! Do you live here, too?"

Patwere shook his head. "No, I have a small house in the village. Heqamaatre does well for himself, though. His family connections bring him a lot of favor — you do know he's the Pharoah's grandson?"

"Yes, I'd heard." Neffi jumped onto the freshly folded cloak and wadded it up to make himself comfortable.

"Not that it makes much difference. There are an awful lot of grandsons. Most of the officials in the Two Lands must be related to the Royal family."

He had a point. Even before his mind began to wander, I think the great Ramesses, himself, had lost track of just how many children and grandchildren he had. I considered making Neffi get off the cloak, then decided against it. "Speaking of relations, I promised a friend I'd look up a cousin of his. A guy named Sahathor. Know him?"

Patwere rolled his eyes then caught himself. "I suppose that isn't a proper response for someone who doesn't know him — Sahathor, I mean."

I grinned. "Don't worry, my friend said his cousin was a character."

Patwere was relieved. "Oh, good. You never know what kind of face someone puts on for their relatives. It doesn't sound like you'll be surprised if I tell you Sahathor is off on one of his benders again."

"Again? I'm amazed he hasn't been sacked by now."

That was the right thing to say. It launched a monologue of gossip, suspicion, and petty complaints that lasted the better part of the hour we spent unpacking. I learned that Sahathor enjoyed his drink a little too much and had a habit of disappearing for days at a time. I also found out that he wasn't called to task for it because the overseer also liked his tipple.

Patwere excused himself just before my companions returned. When I shared my news, Djedmose frowned. "Disappeared on a drunk? That's a problem. When did he go missing?"

"About two days ago. According to Patwere, he ought to be stumbling in any time now. He's rarely gone longer than three days."

Khenemetamun-pa-sheri said, "Missing for days at a time? And no one is upset about this? If it were one of my scribes, I'd be furious." He would, too. Even being late won the offender a good caning.

I shrugged. "Apparently he's Heqamaatre's drinking buddy. They frequently go missing together."

Djedmose's frown deepened. "Prince Merenptah won't be happy to hear that. Nephew or no, he expects Royal appointees to take their responsibilities seriously."

My teacher nodded. "As well he should! A lot can be . . . what's that *cat* doing on my bed?"

We all glanced at Neffi. He was on his back, sound asleep, comfortable in the crumpled embroidery of the older scribe's cloak. Stretched full length, he took up most of the bed.

Djedmose grinned. "He appears to be sleeping, Excellency. Shall I wake him?"

"No. No. No need. It's warmed considerably. I won't need a cloak."

He was wrong. When Patwere came to collect us for the walking tour of the facility, Neffi was still snoring on the cloak. Khenemetamun-pa-sheri made a brave show of being warm in the crisp afternoon sun, but nobody believed him. The goosebumps and chattering teeth were a dead giveaway.

THE CENSUS of the Cattle officially began at sunrise. I accompanied the recording party, making like a dutiful assistant until midday when my teacher told me to get lost. It was Neffi's fault, as usual. He'd taken a liking to the embroidered yoke of Khenemetamun-pa-sheri's cloak and kept climbing him to ride on his shoulders. Sort of makes legible writing difficult.

Time to do what I was there for and look around. Right. Like I knew what to look for. I put Neffi down and he wandered off. Having no better idea, I followed him. He led me into the granaries. I was awestruck by the huge, hive-shaped, mud-brick buildings. Such simple structures, yet they were the lifeline of the nation. Recording their contents figured prominently in the Heb-Sed.

Neffi trotted toward an empty granary, tail swishing. Soon, it would be filled one basket at a time while scribes recorded each load. I suddenly realized Neffi was on top of it now.

He clawed at the bricks, then looked down at me. "Yeow!"

"Neffi! Get down!"

He scratched harder. Bits of brick flew. "EEEE-YOOOOWWW!"

I climbed up and grabbed at him. He eluded me and dug at the other side of the hatch. "What is wrong with you? This place was cleared — even the mice are gone."

"EEEEYOWWW!"

"Leave it!"

Neffi attacked the hatch and I dived for him until finally, I growled, "All right, I'll prove it's empty!" I snatched the handle of the hatch and pulled.

The odor that hit me wasn't the aroma of past grain harvests, but I recognized it, anyway. It was one I hoped never to encounter again. I hastily dropped the lid back into place and crouched, gulping air, until Neffi's face pushed into mine. That cat has smug down pat. "Okay. So it isn't all that empty."

LAMPLIGHT cast distorted shadows on the interior of the granary as Djedmose bent low over the corpse. The man had been dead for several days; and, in spite of the bundles of cloves tied over our noses, we were breathing shallowly. The Medjay topside quit peeking in after the first good whiff. The only one who seemed unaffected was Neffi who was busy inspecting the edges of the floor.

The body probably hadn't been a pretty sight even before decomposition set in. The back of the head was crushed and shards of a beer jar were everywhere. Djedmose rolled the man over and grunted. "Well, kid, you get the job done fast. This is Sahathor, the guy we were supposed to find; but it looks like talking to him is out unless you know a real good magician."

I resituated my cloves. "Don't blame me; Neffi found him. I just opened the lid before he dug through the bricks."

He shot a look over his shoulder. "That cat scares me sometimes. Regardless, we have another problem on our hands. Now we have to find out who killed him."

"Maybe he fell in accidentally and . . . ?"

Djedmose just looked at me.

"Guess not."

Neffi turned his attention to the beaten earth floor where the dead man had lain. I was preparing to shoo him off, when he pounced on something embedded in the dirt and batted it across the floor. It glittered in the dim light as it skittered across the uneven surface. That got Djedmose's attention. "What's he got now?"

Retrieving the object was easier than I expected. Neffi crinkled his eyes and purred as I took it from between his paws. "It's a gold lotus blossom with turquoise insets. Looks like it's from a piece of jewelry."

"Let me see." The Nubian turned the fragment around in his hands and gave a low whistle. "Expensive. Probably from the Royal workshops." Expression unreadable in the shadows, he glanced at Neffi. "We need a chat with Heqamaatre. Grab the Sacred One."

HEQAMAATRE was in his office with Patwere taking inventory of recently-arrived items. The office was large, but seemed cramped due to the number of items awaiting cataloging. Patwere sat cross-legged on the floor in the traditional scribal manner, using his stretched kilt to hold the papyrus. He took one look at Djedmose's face, slid a glance at me, and hastily excused himself.

Heqamaatre was annoyed. "Captain Djedmose, what is the meaning of this? We're already behind schedule."

"Are things going slowly because of your missing scribe?"

"Yes, damn him. He's thrown everything off."

"Then you'll be interested to know we've found him. More precisely: his body. It was found in an empty granary earlier today."

The overseer sat down hard on a gilded chair. It looked more like his legs had quit than a voluntary action. "I see. I'll summon the facility's police chief, then."

"No need, Sir. My men are handling it."

Silence loomed. Djedmose was master of the silent sweat.

So far, they'd ignored me. Fine. I'd planned to let Djedmose do the talking, anyway. Neffi squirmed out of my arms and trotted over to a roll of fine linen, sniffed, then rubbed along its length.

The overseer demanded, "What's that cat doing?"

Djedmose said, "Being a cat, Sir. About Sahathor. I'm a little surprised he'd be missing for days and no one was concerned."

Neffi moved on to a large alabaster vase and stretched against it to sniff the seal covering its mouth. The vase was heavy and didn't even wobble, but Heqamaatre flinched, anyway. I quit watching Neffi and started watching the overseer. He pulled his gaze from Neffi onto Djedmose. "I'm afraid Sahathor was prone to disappearing, Captain. We all thought he'd turn up soon."

"Looks like he has."

Heqamaatre looked sick. Neffi rustled through some scrolls, sneezed, wound around the ornate legs of a folding stool, then disappeared behind a group of chests.

"You haven't asked how he died," Djedmose said.

Trilling, Neffi hopped into sight again onto the top of a large, painted chest. He lay across the lid, batting at the clay seal dangling from the binding cords. It was the Royal Seal.

Heqamaatre jumped up as if prodded with a hot coal. "Get him away from that!"

Djedmose watched Neffi with a raised eyebrow. The cat was now lying on his side pawing at the base of the box. "What's in that chest?"

"Those are items for the Heb-Sed. They haven't been recorded yet."

Neffi was purring loudly, clawing at the crack of the lid. Djedmose said, "Open it, please."

"Impossible. Those items belong to my grandfather, the Pharoah. . . ."

"And I represent the Pharoah. Open the box."

Heqamaatre hesitated, then bent to cut the seal. Neffi dived for the opening lid, but I saw what he was going for before he got there. Over the protests of the overseer, I lifted out a heavy gold pectoral. Its colorful stone and glass inlay glittered as I took the small lotus blossom from my writing kit and fitted it into an almost unnoticeable gap at the bottom edge.

Heqamaatre cried out, "You've broken it!"

Djedmose took the flower and held it up. "It's broken, yes, but Sitehuti didn't do it. We found this piece under Sahathor's body. Any idea how it got there?"

All pretense of self-control fled. Heqamaatre crumpled back into the chair, head in hands. "So much blood. I had no idea there'd be so much blood."

Djedmose stood, head bowed, arms folded in what I recognized as his listening stance. "You better tell me what happened." He didn't have to wait long.

"It was an accident. We were drinking and . . . *why* did he write those damned letters?" Heqamaatre leaned back. "Have you ever seen the goods that come through these storehouses? It's crazy. No one can use all that. We started taking food and wine. Why not? I'm part of the Royal family, right?

"The wine got Sahathor. He loved parties and we threw some great ones. When that got stale, we moved on to bigger items." He shrugged. "I started to enjoy it. It was thrilling to walk away with things and no one was the wiser. Sahathor wasn't like that. All the idiot wanted was to drink and party.

"Heb-Sed goods started coming in. Real nice things. I didn't see a problem with taking a few here and there. Sahathor got scared and wrote a letter to the Royal Overseer.

"I didn't know anything about that until later when we were sharing beer in one of our hideaways. We'd been drinking all day, and I could tell Sahathor was nervous. Finally he told me about the letters. I told him he was a fool.

"He showed me a pectoral from our cache. Said he was going to hand it over as a token of good faith. I couldn't let that happen. I grabbed for it and we fought. He just wouldn't let *go*. Next thing I knew, the beer jug was crashing down . . . he fell and didn't move.

"I panicked and hid the necklace in a chest that just arrived and resealed it. Before I could figure out what to do next, your party arrived."

Silence reigned again. Even Neffi was still, sitting beside the coffer regarding the man with half-closed eyes. Finally Heqamaatre asked, "What happens now?"

A FEW DAYS later, I stood beside Djedmose as his Medjays escorted Heqamaatre onto a boat headed back to the capital. Shoulders slumped, all haughtiness gone, he barely resembled the man who met us on the same docks such a short time before. I wasn't real happy, either.

Djedmose said, "You and the magic cat came through again, kid. Found the thief and solved a murder all at the same time."

"Then, why am I staying here while you're going home?"

"Leave while there's still work to do?" He laughed and swatted me on the back. "Not a chance. You're the assistant to the official scribe of the Census, remember?"

With that, he bounded on board and the crew pushed off. I sat down on the planking next to Neffi, who was stretched full length to absorb all possible warmth, and watched them sail away. When the boat receded far enough I could no longer make out the details of its rigging, I stood and poked Neffi with my toe. "Let's get back to work. This is all your fault, anyway." ✿

T. Lee Harris tells us she grew up in New Albany, Indiana, close enough to the Ohio River that barge whistles and the Belle of Louisville's steam calliope were the background to summer days spent reading Mark Twain, Edgar Allan Poe, Ray Bradbury, and Arthur Conan Doyle. A long-time member of the Southern Indiana Writers' Group, she regularly contributes short stories and artwork to the annual Indian Creek Anthology series.

    While Cat Tales *is her first print publication, other work has appeared online; most recently on* Mysterical-E, *taking first place in the Bloody Groundhog Day contest with the "Maltese Groundhog" (yeah, it has a cat in it, too). When not creating medieval and renaissance constuming or weaving tales with the dubious assistance of six cats, she can be found saving the virtual city of Paragon from pursesnatchers and alien invaders by way of the online game, City of Heroes.*

THE PROBLEM WITH POLLY

by Scott William Carter

IT WASN'T that Nathan Randall disliked cats, but the notion of *liking* them hadn't ever crossed his mind either.

So when he woke to Beethoven's Sonata in F Minor playing from his alarm clock, he stretched out his arms, yawned, and opened his eyes to find this raggedy tortoise-shell cat — an odd jumble of black, tan, and orange fur that made it resemble a gremlin of sorts — staring down at him from atop his dresser, it was cause for concern.

"And what do you think *you're* doing?" Randall said.

The cat blinked.

Randall had a carefully orchestrated schedule. A five minute obstruction would mean five minutes out of his breakfast of tea and biscuits; his brisk walk around the park; his reading of the *Wall Street Journal*; or, worse, tardiness at the Department. He realized that he had left the kitchen window ajar exactly six inches, for it had been a cool evening with a slight breeze, and that this creature must have admitted itself onto the premises through those very six inches.

He rose from bed — swiftly, for Randall abhorred

laziness — and threw on his robe. The cat watched in its own detached way, glancing once at Randall, then drifting its gaze to something else, a smudge on the wall, perhaps, that excited it to the same degree. As Randall looked closer, he noticed that the cat wore a purple collar with a gray metal tag. It was his first sign of good news. Careful not to get too close, he peered at the inscription.

Do not irritate
Do not agitate
This fine furry magistrate
of felicity.

She's one to stay
She's yours each day
If you regard her, as you may
With affinity.

Randall half-suspected that the cat was someone's practical joke; but since he had no enemies, or friends for that matter, he could think of no one who would want to do such a thing. It didn't matter. Regardless of where the animal came from, he had little time for such foolishness. He realized that cats have claws; and those claws, when properly used, could inflict pain. Yet each passing moment was another crimp in his schedule. So without knowing quite what he was going to do, but knowing he had to do something, he reached for the cat.

In one instant the cat transformed itself from a harmless fluff of fur into a screeching, hissing incarnation of the devil. Its back arched, fangs protruded, eyes bulged, and tail shot up. *Do not irritate,* the tag had warned. He saw why.

Now Randall may have been stubborn, but he was no fool who rushed in, so he wisely decided that his hand may not have been the best object in which to shoo away the pugnacious pest. His copy of Dosteveskey's *Crime and Punishment* lay at his bedside, and it being a hardback and at least ten inches in length, might suffice as an instrument with which to prod the cat. This seemed promising in theory, but as he tried it out, poking at the cat, the little creature simply retreated farther back atop his dresser. It hissed defiantly, then proceeded to clean its paws.

"So it's going to be that way, is it, Polly?" Randall said.

He realized that he could solve his problem now, taking whatever time was needed to get the job done, or simply abandon the effort and hope that the cat let itself out. When the cat found that there would be no bowl of milk for its empty stomach, it would seek out another, more yielding host down the street. This is the course of action Randall chose; and later, if he could have done it again, he certainly would have tried harder to rid himself of the cat at that very moment.

For when he returned from his shave and shower, steam rising off his robed body, he found not one cat peering down at him from atop the dresser, but *two*. Two tortoise-shell cats. They sat side by side, identical in every respect right down to the collars and the tags, watching him with the same feline mixture of indifference and indignation. Now Randall knew that he was the target of someone's joke. But who? Who would go to the trouble? Not his boss, for the man may have regarded Randall with reserved contempt, as most people in close contact with Randall did; but he had never overtly harassed him, nor shown any sign that he would. He barely had ten words a day with anyone else at the Department. He never talked with his neighbors.

"Who put you up to this, eh?" Randall asked.

The cats yawned in unison and turned to contemplate lint on the curtains.

It didn't matter. Randall never intended on owning one cat, and he certainly wasn't going to be running a hotel for a whole lot of them. He retreated to the hall closet and retrieved his broom. She yours each day? Not a chance.

He swatted at the twin felines and felt a thrill of satisfaction when the two leapt from their perch and scurried out of the room. He pursued them into the living room, brandishing his weapon as a bloodthirsty conquistador might.

"Run, you little pests! Run! Ha, ha!"

He swatted at their retreating tails. In an instant, the two cats had traversed the distance to the kitchen window. With one last slap at them, Randall succeeded in forcing them outside. He leapt to the window and threw down the sash. Arms raised in victory, he watched the cats disappear under a gap in his wooden fence.

Feeling altogether good about his masculinity, and his heart thundering away in his chest as it hadn't in years, Randall turned back to the bedroom. In one flicker of a cat's whisker, his enthusiasm changed to despair. For there in the living room, lined up across his couch like a row of Roman sentries, were the cats. Not two cats. Not three cats. *Four cats.* Quadruplet Pollys. He felt not anger now, but something else: a darker feeling far removed from his experience.

Dread.

"Now let's think this through," Randall said, although he was talking more to himself than to the cats. "We can work this out."

The cats blinked, eight eyelids snapping in unison, like multiple camera shutters capturing his image.

"I'm going to get dressed for work, you see," Randall said. "Yes, that's exactly what I'm going to do, for I can't be late. I'll leave you to do as you wish. You can think about me. Yes, you can evaluate me for a time, you see. As you can probably tell, I won't be much of a friend to you. Here, I'll even leave the kitchen window open if you should decide to go."

With that, he returned to the bedroom, doing his best to avoid the green eyes of his visitors. His situation did not improve. In the bedroom he found four *more* cats on his dresser, and from the way things had been developing, he knew these weren't the same cats from the living room. In a moment, his suspicion was confirmed, for the cats from before appeared in his doorway.

Then they all meowed, and it was like the blast from a trumpet.

Shaken, Randall proceeded to get dressed. As the

eight watched him, he slipped on his trousers, his perfectly dimpled tie, and his suit jacket. He had a simple plan now. He would ignore them. He would get in his car and go to work. When he returned, they would hopefully have left through the window. No time or appetite for breakfast, he grabbed his car keys and his briefcase and headed for the garage. When he saw his car, however, he knew he wouldn't be leaving any time soon.

It was filled with cats.

Eight of them, it appeared. They covered the driver's seat, the steering wheel, and the dashboard of his gray sedan. Randall felt himself losing it. A burning sensation rose up his neck to his forehead.

"Get out of there, vermin!" he shouted.

Eight more cats appeared in the back seat, their whiskered faces pressed up against the windows. He opened the garage door and found a blockade of cats — *sixteen* of them, he counted quickly — preventing him from leaving. Like a group of finely trained soldiers, they began to march toward him. The car door popped open; and those cats streamed into the garage, joining the others. Their dark fur was like a river of oil flowing in his direction.

He slammed the door and retreated into the house, only to find that the situation inside had worsened. The cats were too many to count. Cats on the refrigerator, the breadbox, the microwave. Cats sitting on the furniture, hiding under it, and hanging from the sides. Cats clawing their way up the curtains. Cats on cats — two or three deep in some places. He could no longer see his carpet, there were so many cats. The shedding hair from so many cats filled the air with thick black smog, and Randall choked and wheezed just to get a breath. He ran for the front door, but when he threw it open, *more* cats poured into the house, blocking his way.

Shielding himself with his briefcase, he retreated in the only way he could — back to his bedroom, for there were yet no cats in that direction. The door to the garage crashed to the floor, and those cats piled into the house. The smell of cats now was overwhelming. Sev-

THE PROBLEM WITH POLLY

eral had already defecated. Others were coughing up hairballs. When they saw that he was moving away, they moved after him — slowly, like a dark blubbering mass of furry lava.

"Get back!" Randall cried.

They arched their backs and hissed, and it was the most frightening sound he had ever heard, like a million bees buzzing through his house. He turned and bolted for the bedroom, and he heard them stampeding behind him. He slammed the door and pressed against it with all his might, but he could feel the pressure building on the other side like a mighty tidal wave, and in an instant the door gave way. His back pressed against his bed, he warded them off by swinging his briefcase, but then they had torn that away from him, and he stood before them, exposed.

Randall fell to his knees. "What do you want from me?"

Fangs out, claws protruding, the cats moved in.

"Please," Randall begged. "I'll do anything."

Several cats in front of him vanished.

What had happened? A cat in front of him was close enough that he could read the inscription on its tag, and the last word of that first stanza — *affinity* — made him realize what he had to do.

"She's one to stay," Randall said. "Of course. *One!* Regard her with affinity."

He wasn't exactly sure how to treat a cat with affinity, but he knew the things most of them liked. He reached out and petted one of them and more of them vanished. Another he scratched behind the ears and the crowd thinned again. They began to purr now, hundreds of them, and if he didn't know better he would have thought it was the first tremblings of an earthquake.

"Good kitty," he said, petting still more. "You're all such good kitties."

Still more cats disappeared, until he could actually see his carpet. He waded through them to his kitchen, for he had an idea of how best to treat a cat like a king. Using the biggest bowl he could find, he poured them nearly an entire gallon of milk and set it down in the middle of a herd. The feeding frenzy lasted only a few moments, and when the milk was gone, only one cat remained.

One scrawny tortoise shell cat. Licking her paws. Ignoring him like only a cat could.

"Hello Polly," Randall said. "Would you like some more milk?"

IT WAS on that day that Nathan Randall became a proud cat owner. He was vigilant in his care for her, never forgetting to put out her food or change her litter box, for if he did he always found that her twins would soon appear. In the mornings, she watched him from the bathroom counter while he shaved, and curled up on his lap while he read the paper. He had to shorten his morning walk by five minutes so as to leave plenty of time for her each morning, but he gladly did so.

It even helped him make conversation with his neighbors and coworkers. For instead of having nothing to say, he now talked about his cat, as all cat owners are prone to do, regaling others who listened with polite attentiveness to his cat's exploits.

He didn't even care when their eyes glazed over. 🐾

Scott William Carter has been a storyteller since the age of seven, when his second-grade teacher published Sucked into Zaxxon, *the riveting, six-page adventure novel that recounted the exploits of a couple of kids transported into an arcade game. Although nothing he has written since has quite given him the same sense of satisfaction as that single-edition book made of cardboard, orange fabric, and clear tape, he has never stopped writing. He has sold over a dozen stories to* Analog, Asimov's, Ellery Queen, Realms of Fantasy, *and* Weird Tales, *as well as to anthologies by Pocket Books and DAW. Recently he has turned his attention to novels — even ones longer than six pages — and his first book,* The Last Great Getaway of the Water Balloon Boys, *has been*

THE PROBLEM WITH POLLY

*published by Simon and Schuster. Born in
Minnesota and raised in Oregon's Willamette Valley,
he continues to make the lush western part of Oregon
his home. Among other things, Scott has been a
bookstore owner, ski instructor, and computer
trainer, but truly realized he was going to make
something of his life when he spent four long nights
picking beets off a conveyer belt at a cannery.
Tolerating his peculiarities on a daily basis are his
patient wife, two young children, two indifferent cats,
a faithful dog, and thousands of imaginary friends.
Find out more about him and his work at his
website: www.scottwilliamcarter.com.*

DELAYED REACTION

by Gareth D. Jones

IN HER dormant state it took a long time for the
massive biolithic creature to react. After unnumbered
centuries the nerve impulses finally reached her petri-
fied brain and passed on the dreadful message: her
nose had been completely sheared off.

Suddenly snapping to full wakefulness, she sprang
to her paws with an agonized howl that was heard
from the Mediterranean to the Red Sea, chilling
the hearts of all who heard. Sand cascaded from her
flanks as she turned and leapt with magnificent feline
grace over the nearest pyramid and vanished into the
hazy heat of the Sahara.   ❧

MRRRAR!

by Edgar Pangborn

TIMMY ate his field mouse, washed, and climbed on a log for a cat's midsummer-night thoughts; black, ten pounds of readiness, no longer young.

Above the house beyond the hayfield a night hawk was rasping. A swaying of trees now and then released the brilliance of village lights a mile away. Down the blind thread of a nearby road swept a noise, with blazing eyes; Timmy ignored it, but tensed at something else appearing on the road — human, it was moving with unhuman quiet, slinking to Timmy's house, crouching at the back door.

Timmy had left through that door two hours ago, by request. Returning, he need only jump on the box outside it and rattle the knob. There would be delays, creaks, moanings — but The Friend would come; it was rarely necessary to wail. The Friend would open up, and say: "Well, damn it . . ."

That human shadow entered the woodshed. Nothing of importance. Timmy relaxed, yawned, and stretched . . .

The Friend used little of the house except the kitchen. His musty cot was there, and a rocking chair where Timmy could sprawl in his lap accepting the caress of crinkled hands, responding with his own baritone purr. It was a good life: Timmy could take it on his own terms.

The shadow was at the door again. A hint of smell with evil association reached Timmy, but it was too faint for complete recognition, and the memory was many days old. . . .

A good life. Compatibility; a supply of milk and mixed-up meat that wasn't bad, and sometimes a sardine; mutual concessions and forbearance. Periodically one of those road-monsters stopped, with one who clattered in to spread mysteries on the table and exchange with Timmy's associate a harmless barking; after this episode something of value usually appeared in Timmy's dish. Few others ever came; when they did Timmy retired under The Friend's cot — except for The Friend he distrusted the tribe.

For one, a slab-faced roarer, he had loathing. Not long ago, The Friend had been engaged in one of his peculiar activities prying up a floor board, lifting a black box, waving away Timmy's nose while the box rustled and jingled. The roarer had arrived during the operation, with uncharacteristic quiet. The Friend had jumped up; the atmosphere was stiff with alarm; Timmy had gone under the cot. But then the intruder had made peaceful sounds, while Timmy studied barnyard-smelling feet and a furry something dangling at the roarer's middle — a rabbit's foot, its odor not quite gone. In time, Timmy had emerged. And without warning the roarer had grabbed his tail, a wet mouth letting off a blast of noise. Timmy had gashed a thick arm and fled in swollen rage while the kitchen boiled, shrillness mingling with the roaring and a slam of the back door. Timmy had not seen the roarer again; once or twice he had caught a whiff of the same stench outdoors, and had hidden in the grass.

The shadow was of no importance. It was only making noiseless motions at the window, lifting it, climbing inside. Timmy stretched again, and wandered into the woods, the best part of the world, his feet touching leaf-mold as an owl's wing touches air.

In a moonless clearing he played make-believe with a pine cone, falling on his side to kick at it, having fun. . . .

by Edgar Pangborn   75

His ears warned him in time to whirl on his back —
hell was loose, on an owl's down-padded wings. Timmy
strove, with teeth and slashing legs — no such rabbit as the owl may have imagined. A hook stabbed;
Timmy yelled, and raked a wild tufted face. The horror let go and vanished in the night.

One talon had bared a rib, going no deeper, but the
gash was painful. Recovering from shock in the safety
of thick brush, Timmy licked it. In due time he crept
slowly home, watchful of the sky. A new thing — trouble had never before come at Timmy out of the sky.
But in his careful passage he had no traffic with imaginary dangers. Timmy met danger as he should: readiness was all.

He jumped to his box. Near the house that faint Bad
Smell now identified itself — slab-faced roarer and no
mistake. But pain and the desire for known shelter
were strongest: the door-knob had to be rattled. Here
was a difficulty: normally the right paw was the knob-
rattling paw, and the wound was on Timmy's right
side. But he made it.

There had been dim sounds of motion in the house;
instead of answering Timmy's application, they
ceased. A dead moment; then a pounding of heavy
steps — away. The front door banged open; feet
thudded up the road. Though alarming, that was all of
secondary importance.

What mattered was that The Friend had to come.
Timmy rattled again; after a decent interval he wailed.
The front door squealed in rising wind, but that was
all. . . . Timmy tried the woodshed: no good.

He considered a window-sill, but his side hurt too
much when he bunched for a leap. At last his forlorn
prowling brought him to the open front door; he trotted through to the kitchen, tail up, calling inquiry. He
sniffed at torn-up floor boards, an empty black box,
and hurried to his dish. It was overturned, but he
licked some comfort from a milk puddle.

The bulk on the cot was the right size for The
Friend. A dangling hand smelled almost right; Timmy
saw it twitch, and arched his neck to rub it. No answering caress, but something tumbled — a rabbit's

THE PROBLEM WITH POLLY

foot on a bit of cord, fastened in some substance with marks on it that clicked as Timmy pushed it. But the atmosphere was wrong for play. Timmy batted the thing idly under the cot, and climbed up.

The bumps and hollows were wrong, unresponsive. Any position troubled the smarting side; Timmy whimpered in exasperation. The Friend was not quite there. Only a pillow at the head end — some spread of white hair above it, but the pillow had the Bad Smell. Timmy returned to his milk puddle: dried up. The front door continued its noise, squeaking and pounding. . . .

A ROAD-MASTER hummed slowly past, stopped, and returned. Brisk footsteps, noise of a voice. Timmy went under the cot.

Below a round white glare in the kitchen doorway Timmy saw legs in a dark shining of leather. These hurried to the cot; the pillow hit the floor. A hand came into Timmy's line of vision, feeling The Friend's fingers, lifting them out of sight. The Leather Legs ran out shouting, returning with another like himself. A spitting flare bloomed into white steady light on the table — The Friend had done that every evening. The object hanging near the back door was jangled: Timmy was used to that — The Friend had often wound the crank as Leather Legs did now, and made noises into it.

One Leather Legs peered under the cot — usual arrangements of pale skin, mouth, nose. He said: "Here, kitty, kitty!" Timmy spat.

The milk dish was righted and filled. A Leather Legs was busy at the table, but his companion stood too near the hall door — no chance to make a break for it yet. Timmy nosed the rabbit's foot, bored.

The table noises were tearing clashes and a moderate "Damn!" — as if The Friend himself were doing the miracle, a miracle now confirmed by the celestial odor and substance of sardine. Beyond the cot Timmy thrust an inquiring face like a black moon. Leather Legs retired. Watching the two with readiness, Timmy accepted. . . . Then the milk. A Leather Legs reached;

Timmy went under the cot. But pain was easing; thirst was appeased; he could wait it out. If The Friend had come back, Timmy might even have made overtures, to the extent of sniffing a shoe-tip. But The Friend did not come back.

Fine night odors were pouring in; The Bad Smell was almost cleaned away. A fox barked, answered by the passion of a dog-voice in the village; the night hawk grated. Timmy worried the rabbit's foot to pass the time.

Poor stuff — no wiggle. A casual flirt of his paw sent it out into the light. A hand swooped down for it with a lively "Hey!"

Timmy didn't mind. What interested him was that now the doorway was clear. A Leather Legs was again booming into the jangling thing.

Timmy ran.

A shout followed him. Actually a human expression of gratitude and esteem, offering an option on a second sardine.

But to Timmy it was only a type of barking. The Friend had gone away.

He watched the sky, traveling slowly but with lessening pain. Trouble, of course, can come from any quarter of the universe: readiness is all. The forest was the best part of the world — there you sometimes even met your own kind.

Timmy said: "Mrrrar. Mrrrar-aorrh?"			🐾

Composer, Army medic, farmer, painter — Edgar Pangborn was all of these, but today he is remembered for his fiction. After collaborating with his sister and his mother Georgia Wood Pangborn (herself a noted author of supernatural fiction) on stories throughout his childhood, Pangborn officially began his writing career with the publication of his first novel in 1930 and spent much of the next twenty years writing mystery and crime stories for the pulp magazine market. In 1951, he turned to writing science fiction, the genre for which he is best-known (Davy, A Mirror for Observers). *His writing over the years has been nominated for a number of awards, and "Mrrraw!," first published in 1953, was one of the winners of the Eighth Annual Detective Short-Story Contest sponsored by Ellery Queen's Mystery Magazine.*

Pangborn continued to write science fiction and mysteries until his death in 1976. In 2003, he posthumously won the third Cordwainer Smith Rediscovery Award, given to writers whose work displays unusual originality and deserves renewed attention.

— Brock James

TWO HAIKU

hearing confession
my cat listens, licks, purrs, and
grants absolution

snubbed on my return
just for one week vacation . . .
fickleness of cats

— Rae Schidlo

HOMING INSTINCT

by Ann Marston

I DIDN'T LIKE the look of the clouds. They were low and black, and spitting moisture that wasn't quite rain. The weather report had warned of scattered thunderstorms over the mountains. Night flying and thunderstorms make a bad combination.

I stood on the ramp, watching the clouds flow across the darkening sky, and I couldn't help thinking about Seth again. It was almost a year ago now that he had taken off from this airport to make the trip across the mountains. He never made the other side, and the searchers never found the aircraft. Seth's slow, warm smile and his blue eyes — brilliantly blue as a September sky — haunted my dreams. I never had the chance to say 'good-bye.' It left everything unfinished, hanging in a strange limbo where I couldn't quite believe that Seth was really dead, but he wasn't nearby to comfort me in my loss.

I guess grief doesn't always have to make sense.

For a moment, I wasn't sure if the moisture on my cheeks was rain or tears. I shook off the fleeting melancholy and walked to the aircraft. The cargo needed checking.

The Twin Otter sat patiently on the ramp in the drizzle. It wasn't the prestigious airline jet I'd once dreamed of flying, or even the sleek corporate jet I would have settled for. The Twin Otter was a workhorse, plain and simple. Built for sheer, dogged endurance and carrying capacity rather than speed and grace, it was reliable and sturdy, utilitarian if not luxurious. It had what Seth referred to as 'beauty of function.' Less than an hour after he introduced me to the airplane, I fell in love with it. It wasn't long after that, I realized I'd also fallen in love with Seth.

The cabin was stuffed to the overhead with cases of tinned food, insulated cartons of frozen foods, and three large wooden crates containing drill bits. I wandered, checking cargo nets and straps. The weight and balance report put us less than three hundred pounds below maximum gross weight. The Tw'otter was not going to be a frisky bird tonight.

The weather briefer said we might run into turbulence in the clouds, and I wanted to make sure the cargo stayed put. Dealing with thunderstorm-related turbulence severe enough to shake the fillings out of teeth is bad enough. A couple thousand pounds of cargo sliding around in the back can become downright discouraging, and it plays havoc with the center of gravity.

Everything looked fine. I double checked, then climbed back down onto the ramp and walked across the wet concrete to the tin-shed airport office.

Tad was by the desk, busy tearing the top three inches off the sides of a styrofoam coffee cup. He filled the remaining shallow tub from a half dozen cream containers scrounged from the coffee room, then he reached under his jacket and pulled out a sodden little ball of grey and black fur. He set it down on the desk by the truncated cup.

"What in the hell is that?" I asked.

Tad turned, startled. He looked like a kid caught with a pocketful of the next door neighbor's apples. He grinned sheepishly at me.

"It's a cat," he said. "Poor little thing's starving."

I stepped around him to get a closer look. The little grunge ball on the desk might have been a kitten, but it looked more like a half-drowned rat. It was barely half grown, and it was the scrawniest damned thing I've ever seen in my life. It crouched on the desk, face plunged into the cup, little pink tongue making short work of the cream. Its grey-and-black fur, sticking out in spikes, looked moth-eaten and couldn't disguise the sharp ridge of its shoulder blades. A sad little apology for a tail lay limp on the desk, half curled around the dirty paws. It finished the cream, nearly knocking over the cup trying to get the last drop.

Tad pulled another handful of cream containers from his jacket pocket. The kitten watched with rigid intensity as he refilled the empty cup. It looked up at him, as if asking permission to continue. Tad grinned and nudged the bony little bottom, urging the cat closer to the cup. It didn't need a second invitation.

"I found him in the hangar," Tad said. He scratched the scraggly grey fur behind the cat's ear. The ear flicked, and the cat made a quick, rusty buzzing sound, but remained devoted to the task at hand.

The cat finished the last of the cream and sat up straight on the desk, front paws placed neatly together, afterthought of a tail wrapped around the paws with an air of incongruous dignity. It looked up at me. Its eyes were a deep, vivid shade of blue, clear as mountain lakes under an autumn sky.

I took a closer look at it, and realized suddenly that it wasn't a grey and black cat. It was merely covered in grease and oil. So not only scrawny, but filthy, too.

As if in response, the cat lifted one paw and licked it, then smoothed the grimy paw across the side of its cheek. It didn't seem to do much good.

"He's white, I think." Tad picked it up. "Give him a bath, put a little meat on his bones, and he'll be a real pretty little thing." The kitten nestled into the crook of his arm and began purring, producing enough volume to vibrate its fur. Its whole body trembled in ecstasy as it kneaded the inside of Tad's elbow. Tad grinned and glanced up at me sideways, like a little kid. "I thought we might keep him."

"Keep it?" I said. "Like take it with us? Not a chance, kid." I placed my index finger firmly on his chest for emphasis. "I'm not having a cat on my airplane."

"C'mon, Lucy," he said. "He doesn't weigh much more than half a pound or so. He'll sleep most of the way home. If we leave him here, he'll starve."

Still purring, the cat looked up at me. I don't like cats. They're entirely too self-centred and arrogant for me. I get the impression they believe human beings are too far beneath them to notice — except of course when it's time for dinner.

"You'll hardly know he's there," Tad said. "Besides, every airplane needs a cat."

I raised an eyebrow. Tad had a quick and slightly off-center imagination. Justifying that last comment might take all of it. "It does, huh?"

"Sure. You know. Cat-and-duck method of IFR flight."

"Cat and —?" Then I recognized the old joke. If all the gyros failed in the clouds, the cat, having its own internal gyros and always landing on its feet, would show the pilot how to keep the wings level. As for the duck — ducks always land safely, so the pilot just tossed it out the window and followed it down. Another one of those ideas that work far better in theory than in practice.

"Yeah, right," I said. He raised his eyebrows and smiled at me in that way he has, and he knows I have a hard time resisting. I sighed, defeated. "Well, okay, then. But if that thing makes a mess in my airplane, you're cleaning it up."

"I'll get a box and some newspaper." He grinned and scratched the cat's ears again. "Besides, white cats are good luck. They're the special children of Bast."

"Bast?"

"Yeah. The Egyptian cat goddess. Or they're returned spirits. Pick whatever legend you want."

"I'll leave the legends to you. Go check the weather again, and do the walk around. I'll meet you at the airplane in about twenty minutes."

The cat chose that moment to leap out of Tad's arms. Still purring like a finely tuned Pratt & Whitney PT6 engine, it weaved itself around my ankles, leaning well into the turns like a good pilot, and flowing like liquid around my feet. It gave me an oddly pleasant sensation in my chest, and I nearly reached down to scratch its ears.

"Let's go do as the lady says, Cat." Tad scooped up the cat and hoisted it to his shoulder. Cat crouched there, his tiny claws deep in the fabric of Tad's jacket. He looked determined to hang on, settling in for the duration.

WE HAD FLIGHT-PLANNED for a trip of a little under three hours. During the day, in clear weather, the scenery was spectacular over the mountains. At night, in cloud, it always made me feel a bit edgy. We'd be flying at ten thousand feet. Our route gave us fifty miles horizontal distance from peaks stretching up to over twelve thousand feet. I trusted the radio nav aids to keep us on course and well away from all that vertical real estate to either side. That's a lot of trust to put in a bunch of electronic gadgets. The pilots' term for mountain peaks hidden in cloud was *cumulo-granite*. Hitting one could ruin your whole day.

Is that what happened to you, Seth?

I let the thought go and strapped myself into the left seat, settling my headset over my ears. With Cat still clinging to his shoulder, Tad read the items off the checklist. I had started the Twin Otter often enough so that I could do it in my sleep, but company policy insisted on following the checklist religiously. It was a good procedure. Habit was unreliable, a fact proven too many times when pilots accidentally took off with incorrect flap settings, or fuel selectors sitting blithely on empty tanks.

The engines started smoothly, all the engine gauges sitting firmly in the green. Tad set all the communication and navigation radios as I taxied to the end of the runway. He announced our intention to take off. Nothing disturbed the slight hiss of static in my headset to indicate conflicting traffic. Even as I reached up to advance the throttles, I craned forward to take a good look around the sky, searching for red and green navigation lights. Some aircraft still went around with no radios. Nordo, we called them. Perfectly legal, but they could cause a nasty shock if you didn't check for them. The sky seemed clear so we moved out onto the threshold of the runway and I pushed the throttles forward for full power.

Six hundred feet off the deck, we were in the cloud. The cat on Tad's shoulder watched me with great interest as I attended to all the routine little chores to ensure a smooth climb to altitude. I turned to reach up over my shoulder for the switch to test all the warning lights once more, and caught Cat looking at me again, his blue, blue eyes narrowed to slits. For a second, I could have sworn he grinned at me in approval. Then he closed his eyes and settled into a scruffy little ball. His purr was a warmly comforting sound in the cockpit.

WE HIT THE TURBULENCE an hour and a half into the flight. It started out as mild chop, not much worse than driving an old stiff-suspensioned pickup over a wash-boarded country road. Tad and I tightened our seatbelts. Cat sat up and yawned, then began washing with elaborate nonchalance. He didn't make much headway against the grease and oil staining his fur. All he succeeded in doing was spreading the stuff in a thinner layer over a wider area.

A bolt of lightning lit the sky with eerie blue light. At the same time, the airplane dropped five hundred feet like an express elevator heading for the basement. Maps, pens, and flashlights hung in the air for a second, weightless, then showered down onto my shoulder and arm. It felt like slamming into concrete when we hit the bottom of the downdraft. The next second, the Tw'otter lurched sideways to the left, tilting the wings nearly perpendicular to the ground.

"Get that wing up," I shouted, grabbing the yoke with both hands. My foot shoved the right rudder pedal all the way to the floor. I felt Tad's foot hit his pedal an instant after I stomped mine. It took both of us to wrestle the aircraft back to wings level.

An updraft caught us. The force of it pushed my head down against my shoulders, made my feet too heavy to stay on the rudder pedals. The nose pitched up; and the left wing came up, pointing straight at the sky. The attitude indicator in front of me toppled, making it completely useless as a reference for keeping the wings level. Something in the cabin behind us creaked alarmingly.

The airspeed indicator unwound like a broken spring. In about three seconds, the Tw'otter was going to stall and snap off into a spin, then fall out of the sky like a broken duck. I pushed forward on the column with all my strength. Tad jammed the right rudder pedal all the way to the floor. The airplane shuddered and trembled, but the nose came down and the wings levelled.

For a moment, we flew straight and level. I wiped the sweat from my forehead and glanced at Tad. He was as pale as I felt, both of us sweating and a bit breathless. Cat clung to his shoulder with the claws on all four feet dug in deeply, pupils black and round inside a ring of vivid blue, showing no sign of the panic I expected. He was uncannily calm, his small body swaying easily and automatically to compensate for the jerky movement of Tad's shoulder with the turbulence, spindly little tail acting as a rudder.

The sky lit again with another flash of lightning. Blue, twisting ropes of electric fire danced around the nose of the aircraft, coiling and tangling around the wings and the engines, lacing through the prop arcs like streams of molten sapphire. The burst of static in my headset nearly deafened me. It lasted only an instant, then was gone, leaving not so much as the hiss of a carrier wave. The cockpit lighting went out.

I snapped on the feeble, battery-powered overhead light, then reached for the flashlight, fingers scrabbling on the deck by my feet. The Tw'otter lurched again, nose down to the right this time. I found the flashlight, but didn't have time to turn it on. Tad shouted something, wrestling with the yoke and rudder pedals. I grabbed the yoke. We pulled back, struggling to bring the wings level and the nose up. The g-force pinned me down in my seat. It took all my strength to raise my arm and pull the throttles back.

A deep, shuddering thump wracked the airframe. For one heart-stopping second the control yoke went limp in my hands. Then the wings came level. Between us, Tad and I managed to get the nose up and keep the aircraft more or less straight. But we could do nothing about the altitude. The turbulence tossed us about like a cork in white water rapids.

I watched the airspeed indicator in horrified fascination. The needle blurred around the face of the instrument, bouncing back and forth between forty knots and two hundred knots too quickly to see. The Twin Otter should have been falling out of the sky in a dead stall. Or breaking up into small pieces. Incredibly, it did neither. I didn't have time to wonder about it. Besides, it doesn't pay to question miracles.

Then, without warning, we were out of the turbulence and into calm air. Stunned, Tad and I sat there, staring at each other in the dim light. I switched on the flashlight. Both of the gyros — attitude indicator and heading indicator — were still toppled and useless, struggling to erect themselves. The turn coordinator, an electric gyro, still worked. Automatically, I glanced up at the magnetic compass. Something hard must have hit it, perhaps the flashlight as it sailed through the air. The glass bowl was shattered, the clear kerosene spilled away onto the deck. The compass card swung aimlessly, tilted drunkenly to the right.

A cold chill rippled down my spine. We were in the middle of the mountains at eight thousand, three hundred feet in the clouds, with no reliable way of knowing which direction we were going. All around us, peaks soared to twelve thousand feet. Both the navigation and the communications radios were dead. We had no way of telling where the peaks were.

"Can we climb?" Tad asked, his voice loud in the silence.

The yoke still felt strange — loose and spongy, as if something had snapped between it and the elevator. When I reached up to push the throttles forward, a bone-deep shudder wracked the aircraft. The airspeed fell off alarmingly and the right wing threatened to drop. Hastily, I shoved the nose down and pulled back the throttles.

"Feels as if we damaged something back in the tail," I said. "It's not going to climb."

He looked ahead through the windscreen at the ghostly grey emptiness out there. He grinned wryly. "Wonder how long it will be before we hit something."

The question needed no answer, but I nodded in acknowledgment. *Would it be so bad? Would it bring Seth and me together again?*

Cat made a soft little noise, not quite a miaow, not quite a growl. The raspy little chirrup sounded strangely like a question. He leaped from Tad's shoulder onto the top of the glareshield, then paced the length of it until he was in front of me. He turned to look back over his shoulder. Those blue eyes stared directly into mine for a moment, mesmerising me. I couldn't look away.

Finally, he walked back to the centre of the glareshield and sat down, peering intently through the windscreen. Tad and I exchanged glances. Tad shrugged.

Cat sat there quietly for several minutes. Suddenly he sprang to his feet, scrawny little body hunched into a scruffy little arch. His fur stuck out in oily spikes and he hissed and spat, glaring to the right.

I looked past Tad, out the right window. I saw nothing, but on sudden impulse, I twisted the yoke to the left.

"Jesus, Mary, and Joseph!" Tad whispered in awe.

I glanced to the right just in time to see the ghost of something pale and solid slide past the up-tilted right wing. My heart tried to leap right out of my chest through my throat.

Cat resumed his seat in the centre of the glareshield, again peering forward.

Tad looked at me, pale as the granite wall we had just missed. "I don't believe that," he said.

Cat looked back over his shoulder at me. I could swear he grinned before he turned his attention back to the sweeping banks of swirling cloud beyond the windscreen. A moment later, he bounced up, hissing and spitting, scowling out the right side window again.

"This is ridiculous," I muttered. But I didn't hesitate to turn to the left. I didn't see anything out the window this time. Cat resumed his seat.

"What was the weather to the west of the mountains?" I asked, more for something normal to say than with any hope we'd actually make it that far.

Tad retrieved his clipboard and glanced at his notes. "Ten thousand thin scattered, and there should be a full moon."

"Good VFR, then," I said absently, watching Cat.

Cat got to his feet and casually walked to my side of the glareshield. He looked at me calmly, then put up a paw to touch the windscreen post. His eyes looked like mountain lakes. Seth's eyes were that color. Cat blinked.

I banked slightly to the left. Cat sat there for another moment, then walked back to the centre. I levelled the wings. He lay down and began purring.

This couldn't be happening, could it? I couldn't be sitting here, flying an airplane under the direction of a small, scraggly white cat. Things like this just aren't for real, are they? Maybe we had hit a mountain, and we were all dead and just didn't know it yet.

"Don't question miracles," I muttered under my breath. Tad gave me a lop-sided grin and nodded his agreement.

Twenty minutes later, we burst out into clear air. Below us, the mountains fell off sharply into rolling foothills. The moon turned the landscape to pale silver. Ahead, the lights of a town glimmered and sparkled against the shadowy trees. Cat yawned mightily, then curled up and went to sleep on the glareshield.

THE ENGINEER came into the office, shaking his head. He flopped into a chair opposite the leather couch where Tad and I sat, cradling cups of hot coffee in hands that still trembled slightly. Cat sat primly on the low table in front of the couch, scruffy little tail wrapped around his paws.

"You two had a whole squadron of guardian angels working overtime for you tonight," the engineer said. "The right wing is twisted a couple of degrees off true, and there's eight rivets popped in the tail. There ain't one electric working in the whole airplane. With luck like that . . ." He shook his head again, then got to his feet. "Well, you made a lot of work for me. I better get started."

Cat stood up and stretched. As the engineer left, Cat leaped from the table to my knee, then onto my shoulder. He settled into a small curl against the side of my throat, and the comforting rumble of his purr vibrated against my skin.

Tad looked at Cat for a long moment, then met my gaze and grinned. "You've been adopted," he said. "I'd say you've got yourself a cat."

"He's your cat," I said, but made no move to dislodge the furry little bundle.

Tad laughed softly. "You sure don't know much about cats," he said. "He's made up his mind that you're his people. You can't argue with that."

I reached up and scratched Cat's ear, remembering Tad's words about legends. Wasn't there also something about white cats being returned spirits? I smiled, still stroking the oily white fur. Suddenly, I didn't feel so achingly alone any more. 🐾

I've spent most of my life being owned by airplanes and cats, but not necessarily in that order. I've worked as a flight instructor, an airline pilot, and an airport manager. My published works include the Rune Blade Trilogy *and the* Sword in Exile Trilogy, *both published by HarperCollins. I've had short stories appear in* The Return of the Dinosaurs, Zodiac Fantastic *and the SF/F magazine* On Spec. *I'm currently working on two new novels. I live in Canada and am at present sharing my life with Friend, the World's Prettiest Calico, and Stormy, seven pounds of cat and fourteen pounds of hair.*

PRINCESS OF SOZOPOL

by Anna Sykora

I FOUND MRS. MILEVA'S house in Sozopol at the end of a cobblestoned alley, where the smallest car would have gotten stuck. Built like its neighbors of dark-varnished wood, it had a cat-size balcony, all glassed in; and on it sat a cream-colored Persian. She sat so still on her satin pillow, staring straight ahead through her rusted grill, I thought she was stuffed (I've read about pet lovers who can't let go). Then she blinked.

Unshouldering my pack, I tidied my long hair with my fingers and rang the bell: no answer. I rapped on the door, and a woman in a flowered kerchief made the gesture of throwing something down.

"Please, has Mrs. Mileva gone away?" I asked in English.

She chuckled, disclosing a steel front tooth. "Mileva . . ." She tapped the side of her head, and my heart sank as she trotted away.

Suddenly the door pulled open, and a tiny woman peered up at me, her thin grey braids arranged in a circle like a crown. She fell back a step, her features working.

"What is it?" I cried, and she shook her head yes — which means 'no' in Bulgarian. Tears showed in her eyes; getting a grip, she asked me with a note of disapproval: "Miss Irene Duke? I really did not expect you till this evening." Her clear British English came as a surprise.

"I'm sorry, I took an earlier bus. I tried to call you."

"Please, come in. Is that all your luggage?" She nodded at my heavy pack.

"Yes. Please call me Irene."

"Do you always carry your own things, Miss Irene?"

"I find it's easier."

"Modern girls," she muttered, and I followed her inside. Little paintings of landscapes lined the hall, above delicate bits of furniture. Everything looked tidy and tired.

"Your room is upstairs." Pausing at the stairs, which were steep, she took a deep breath. "At present you are my only guest. You'll find this house is very quiet."

"Good, I've got a pile of work to do."

"I assumed you were a tourist, Miss Irene. You'll find the sea still warm enough for bathing."

I just nodded, and she led me up two creaking flights of stairs, to a musty room under the roof, with a bedstead of cast iron. At least it had a view of the beach below the house, where a dock without boats jutted into the smooth, blue sea.

"You may have your breakfast anytime after 7 A.M.," she said crisply. "Just come downstairs and I will get it. I don't have any help at present."

"I'm sure I'll feel comfortable here. Your English is excellent."

"I used to teach English," she confided, "though I never was able to travel outside. In the old days the rules were different. We were not so free." She peered again at my contoured pack, decorated with stickers from all over Europe.

"You have a beautiful cat," I said. "I saw her on her balcony."

"Princess is a cat of the houses, not the streets. You must never let her leave this house."

"I understand. I love cats."

THAT NIGHT, as I was tossing on my lumpy bed, a motorcycle growled near the house. A door slammed, and heavy footsteps made those old stairs groan. A voice complained rudely in Bulgarian, and I heard Mrs. Mileva pleading. Then a door shut, and the house grew quiet.

Seagulls kept crying plaintively. I thought of my grandmother on the run, maybe cowering in this room, waiting for a rapping on the door — the police, to drag her away.

THE NEXT morning, over stale rolls and watery coffee in the kitchen, I asked my hostess: "Is there another guest? I heard someone come in last night."

"That man's not a guest," she said curtly, pouring me more coffee unasked from an enameled pot. Her frail hand was shaking.

"He lives here?" I asked innocently.

"From time to time. I didn't expect him. Now he's out on his rotten boat again, the *Freedom*. I hope it sinks!"

Abruptly she bustled away; Princess was meowing in the living room. The man must be an awkward relative, I thought; my hostess felt ashamed of him.

THE DAY looked bright, and I love to swim, so I had a long workout in the warm and waveless water. In early October, deserted by the crowds, the Black Sea's a great big swimming pool. Except for one red-cheeked grandpa, shepherding three kids who were collecting shells, I had the strip of white-sand beach to myself.

Too lazy to get back to work (I'd brought my laptop down), I was sunning myself when I heard a heavy motor cutting out. A dirty old boat softly bumped the dock, *Swoboda* [*Freedom*] painted on its prow in Cyrillic letters. Stepping from the cabin, a powerfully built and sun-bronzed man flung a rope around a piling. I noticed a snake tattoo coiled around his heavy forearm.

Shaking back his long, loose black hair he grinned at my red bikini, and called out something in his language. I shook my blonde head "no," then remembered this means "yes." Tying up his boat, he soon came swaggering towards me, carrying a wooden box of tackle. As he passed, he gave me a lingering once-over, and I just stared back.

Now I'm pretty well built, and keep myself fit, and I've known some unusually good-looking guys try to deck me with their gaze. This man made my heart speed up; but sitting in the sun I shivered too: striding up the beach he scattered those kids like birds, as if he enjoyed it. Their grandpa plucked up the smallest girl, and chiding the intruder over his shoulder, hurried away with them in the other direction.

Mrs. MILEVA'S furnishings looked as if they'd sat undisturbed for a hundred years. I thought she might remember things that would help me with my book. So when she invited me to tea, in the living room, I was glad to accept.

"You are my first American guest," she said, offering me a silver plate of crescents frosted with confectioner's sugar. "How did you ever find me?"

"Through the internet. You know, the computer system."

"I don't know anything about such things."

"An agency had listings of bed-and-breakfasts. I wanted to stay out on the peninsula."

"In our Old Quarter. Why is that, Irene?" She took a tiny bite of cookie.

"I'm working on a book." Her blue eyes flashed, and I saw my stock was rising. Eastern Europeans still read books and honor writers.

"Is that so? You seem so young for an author."

"I'm taking a year off after college, before I go to graduate school. I need to work on this project before the witnesses all are . . ."

"Dead?" she queried, sitting up very straight at the antique table.

"My Bulgarian grandmother, who was a Jew, fled the country in 1943. I'm retracing her steps. She found refuge for a week in Sozopol, she told me, somewhere right in this neighborhood."

"How interesting." Mrs. Mileva bestowed a measured smile. She still had her own teeth, like yellowed pearls. "Do you know, my own mother might have sheltered her." Getting up, she fetched a dented box embossed with the portrait of a crowned man in a uniform trimmed with gold braid. Prying off the cover, she rummaged in a heap of decaying photos and selected one.

"This is my mother." A plump woman with piled dark braids smiled smugly into the camera. "I was just a little girl in the war. I don't remember much; I try not to remember. Sometimes Mother was hiding people. She put them up where Borislav sleeps."

"In that shed near the beach?" He'd left the door open, and I'd seen his cot and his tackle box.

"Yes. Your grandmother would have been safe."

"Before she died, she said she never felt safe, after Bulgaria joined the Nazis."

Mrs. Mileva frowned.

"Your mother was very beautiful," I added quickly.

"We are distant relatives of Boris III — our king the Nazis killed." Dreamily she smiled, and I wondered if this was the truth. Her neighbor had warned me with the universal sign for crazy people.

When Princess came meowing to our feet Mrs. Mileva picked her up and draped her around her neck. The heavy beige cat just hung there, dangling her fuzzy paws.

"Once I had many furs to adorn me; now this is my only one. Once I had a beautiful daughter too. She was just your age when she — went away." Getting up, holding the cat's paws together like the ends of a shawl, she brought me a faded photo in a heart-shaped, silver frame. A shapely young woman in a broad-brimmed hat leaned against a tree, in profile. Gazing away with a mournful expression she held up one white rose. She looked like me, I had to admit — play-acting in old-fashioned clothes. Then again, I'm half Bulgarian.

"Did I surprise you at the door?"

"I thought my Irina had come home." My hostess patted her eyes with her napkin. "It is impossible; she is dead."

Just then Borislav came bursting in, and Princess fled to her balcony's shelter. Stopping short, he glared at me.

by Anna Sykora   95

"Do not leave me, Irene," Mrs. Mileva urged in English. "You are my guest; I invited you to tea." She muttered something in Bulgarian that sounded like a warning, but bending over her he spat insulting words. Clenching her eyes, she turned her face away; and I was starting to get up, when grabbing her teacup he threw it into the fireplace — smash!

We sat in shock as he crossed the room and pulled out a drawer in her slender-legged desk. Rifling through it, he pocketed a wad of bills. Then he left us, slamming the door so hard a little painting of roses dropped from the wall.

The color drained from the old woman's face, and she pressed a fist to her heart, gasping:

"Give me my pills, dear — in the desk. The open drawer!"

I rushed to obey. Her prescription vial held four pills, and she swallowed one. I brought her a glass of water, and in a minute she was breathing easier.

"Nitroglycerine," she said, calmly getting up to put the vial back. "I have a heart condition, which he knows. He only makes it worse for me, the brute."

"He does seem cruel, . . ."

"I only tolerate him because he is all that remains of my daughter. Yes, Borislav is my grandson — though no one can see a resemblance. He is tainted by his gypsy blood! His father seduced and stole my daughter, when she was still an innocent girl. He ruined her; she died from his abuse — and now the young one blames me for *his* death, but Irina, I assure you . . ." Hot color burned in her cheeks, and I thought she'd die before my eyes.

"Mrs. Mileva, you should rest," I told her firmly. "I'll take our tea things back to the kitchen." I helped her to her armchair near the fireplace, where she sat stiffly, audibly breathing, still clutching her daughter's portrait.

Fussing in the kitchen with the dishes — there was no dishwasher — I felt embarrassed and perplexed. This family had real problems. I was just a visitor, however. I'd come in search of my grandmother's life, only to get sucked into a darker drama.

On the other hand, I'd paid for my whole week in Sozopol in advance. The Old Town was thick with atmosphere; I'd seen donkey-carts loaded with firewood, and old men sawing wood by hand. Their wives sat in chairs in the sun outside their houses, stitching away at exquisite embroideries, which they hoped to sell to tourists. If I stayed, I thought, I might better imagine how my grandma had survived the war. She too had depended on strangers, as she made her way alone towards the Turkish border, walking all the way, carrying her carpetbag, sleeping in barns and haystacks . . .

"Thank you dear, you have been very kind," Mrs. Mileva murmured, as I brushed the crumbs from her table.

"Can I do anything else for you?"

"No, I will rest. . . . Can you bring me Princess, dear?"

I lifted the heavy cat from the pillow on her glassed-in balcony. The satin pillow was embroidered with a crown, neatly worked in gold metallic thread. Gratefully taking Princess into her lap, Mrs. Mileva caressed her creamy-beige fur.

"My best friend," she crooned. "Princess will never leave me all alone."

I felt a pang, as if she reproached me, mixing me up with her long-lost daughter. "Are you sure you don't want me to call a doctor?"

"No, I have lived many years with my bad heart. I know what to do."

"Then thank you for the tea," I said awkwardly. "And your vanilla cookies were delicious."

"A recipe from my mother, dear."

I left her in her armchair with her cat, and the photo of the girl who'd run away.

THAT WAS the last time I saw her alive. When my alarm peeped, at 7 A.M., I heard no footsteps on the stairs, no clinking or clattering from the kitchen. Downstairs, Princess started to meow, plaintively, insistently. I took a quick shower, dressed, and ventured down.

As soon as I opened the living room door, she shot past me and galloped up the stairs. The room was still dark, its shutters closed. Frightened, I groped for a light — and saw my hostess slumped in her armchair, her head twisted to one side, her mouth sagging half-open. One of her braids hung loose on her cheek, and I felt sad for her to be seen this way.

She must have had a second, more violent attack. I checked the drawer in her rosewood desk. There lay the vial, with three pills; she'd had no time to take another.

Then I noticed something odd in the tidy room. (I'd hung the painting back on the wall, and swept the broken china from the fireplace). The cat's pillow on her miniature balcony showed no crown: it was upside down. Hardly knowing what I did, I turned it over, and caught my breath: three long, grey hairs adhered to the golden embroidery. Borislav — who'd stripped his grandma's cash — had suffocated her, with this pillow!

I ran into the street; I cried for the police; I pulled two frightened neighbors into the house, to show them my dead hostess. Eventually, with the help of a young boy proud of his English (he started every sentence with 'Good morning'), I got one overweight and sleepy-looking cop to venture into the house.

"I be Cal the Police," he announced, tapping his side-of-beef chest. Speaking slowly and clearly, I explained I'd been staying in Mrs. Mileva's house. Politely he listened, then gave her body just a cursory look.

"She was old, with bad heart." He made a falling motion with his plump hand. "It was her time, you see."

"What do you think of these hairs on this pillow?" I demanded, thrusting it into his face. "Plus, it was on the cat's balcony upside down — with the crown underneath. Mrs. Mileva was always so tidy. I drank tea with her here in this room last night, and I swear this pillow was right side up."

"Old people get funny," he said blandly. "In Sozopol are many funny old people."

"But where is her grandson, Borislav? He sleeps here sometimes, on a cot in the shed. I bet he had a motive to kill her and make it look like natural causes. He's probably her only family; I bet he inherits this house himself. I saw him take her money last night."

"Miss, do you read your Agatha Christie?" Officer Cal asked slyly.

"Yes, but that has nothing to do with this case!"

"I think you read too many stories, Miss. Now please pack your thing and leave this house."

"O.K.," I said, resentfully. "You're the law in Sozopol. But what about Mrs. Mileva's cat? She has an old Persian named Princess."

"You can feed it, if you like; I will not seal this house today. It is not a scene of crime. You please to leave your key with the neighbor lady."

"Who will take care of Princess?"

"We will find someone, or take her to the shelter." He studied the floor.

"She's a very old cat; you can tell from her teeth."

"Miss, I think she is not your problem." Two solemn-faced men stepped in with a stretcher. "Now please, go pack your thing."

Reluctantly, I left the room: Borislav would get away with murder.

PRINCESS WAS hiding under my bed, inside my empty pack. Meowing at me reproachfully, she stared up at me with her soulful brown eyes, then rubbed her silky face against my hand. When I lifted her into my lap, she snuggled and purred, closing her eyes. I felt very sorry for her. I sat and thought, then nestled her onto my pillow.

Fetching her dry food from the kitchen, I fed her from a bowl in my room. The men had already gone.

"I can't leave you with these unfeeling people," I told her while she munched. "Let me go get some pizza; then we'll head for the bus together. There's room in the top of my pack."

The *Swoboda* was bobbing at the dock, but I saw no sign of Borislav. I felt sure he'd quietly slipped away, and would stay lost till I left town.

At a snack bar I learned all the buses were on strike. Maybe they'd run in the morning again. Yes, I could take a taxi to Burgas, but it would be very expensive.

Not wanting to pay for a taxi, I made a decision that

almost cost two lives: I'd stay in the house with Princess for one last night. Frankly, I had another motive: I wanted to look through Mrs. Mileva's photos. Maybe I'd find a clue to my grandma's trek, or at least a detail for my story about her.

WHEN I got back, I found the food and water untouched that I'd left for Princess. Worried, I searched in every room, calling her name and shaking her box of dry food. Why was she hiding from me now, when she'd turned to me for help? I didn't want to leave her alone — with Borislav.

Rain started to pelt the old wooden house; even the after-season was ending. Soon only the elderly locals would be left in the quaint Old Quarter — with a murderer moving among them.

Opening the box with the king's portrait, I felt guilty. Quickly I sifted through my hostess's photos; and soon enough found one of her mom smiling at a man in a Nazi uniform. His collar bore the double **S** of Hitler's worst fanatics. My hostess had been telling me a tall tale about her mother hiding Jews. . . .

Suddenly I heard a heavy tread, and froze with the photo in my hand. Looming up in the doorway, Borislav laughed out loud. His cheeks were stubbly, his eyes bloodshot, and I could smell his winy breath a yard away.

"Liars and pigs, these women," he growled as I dropped the photo back into the box. "Yelena's mother was a Ratnik, who loved Nazis. Later Yelena, she tell stories of my father to the Communists, for revenge. She thinks he stole my mother away, but she made him to die in the prison — Yelena killed my father!"

Leaning over me he leered, and I shuddered, then looked him straight in the eye:

"Where's Princess?"

"What, you care?"

"I wanted to take her with me tomorrow."

"I threw her out already. This my house. It all is mine."

"You killed Yelena, didn't you? Suffocated her with the pillow."

Harshly he laughed as I leaped for the door, and then grabbed me by my hair, and slammed me against the wall. . . .

PUTT-PUTT-PUTT. . . . A motor throbbed in the side of my head; painfully throbbed, reeked of diesel. Gagged with a gritty rag, roped up tight, I lay on my side on the rocking floor. Behind me a loud voice hoarsely sang, "Exit light, enter night . . ." from Metallica. I kept my eyes shut and lay dead still, though my wrists and ankles ached, and I couldn't feel my feet. This nightmare was real: I was a prisoner on the *Swoboda*.

When Borislav killed the motor, I started to shake; I couldn't stop. The boat pitched gently, and my stomach churned as his footsteps thudded near. Chuckling he knelt behind me and rolled me on my back, then lightly slapped my cheeks. Cupping my breasts he squeezed them hard:

"Say your prayers, little one." His deep-set eyes burned into mine, and his hot breath smelled so sour. Glowering, I yelled through my gag — an animal's cry — and he just laughed. Ripping open my blouse, he tore it to rags and stripped them off my body. I writhed and bucked and tried to fight, but he pulled down my pants and underpants together, to my shins. Then he fumbled with the ropes on my ankles he'd tied so tight he couldn't unknot them.

Cursing, he wallowed towards his tackle box; but when he opened the lid, the cat jumped out, all filthy and bedraggled. He kicked at her and missed, then threw open the cabin's door and pointed at the night. Out scurried Princess, but he followed, snatching up a gaff.

Scrambling up I hopped towards his box; but a heave of the boat overturned me; and I fell headlong, banging my forehead on the deck. Blood filled my eyes, but I shook my head; in the tackle's strew lay a rusty knife; and seizing it I frantically sawed two-handed at the ropes on my ankles.

When Princess came panting back inside, with the killer at her heels, I snatched her up and threw her in his face! She hung by her claws from his cheeks while he howled, and I struggled with the ropes on my hands. Tears and blood dripped down my face; just in time I worked my right hand free — and as he wiped her away, and plunged at me, I stuck that knife right in his thigh.

Bellowing, he fell on his knees, and I staggered through the door, pulling off my gag and kicking off the stumble of my clothes. Princess stood gasping on the edge of the gunwale, and I grabbed her and jumped overboard. Turning on my back I kicked for my life in the warm dark sea. Her claws got entangled in my bra; and she scratched me, crying like a frightened baby; so I squeezed the back of her neck pretty hard. Her body went limp, and she shut up. Thank God for the kitten reflex, which lets a mother cat carry her child silently out of the reach of danger.

Borislav was cursing and thumping around, trying to restart his rickety motor. I swam strongly in a line away from his noise, into the dark, into the mist, gripping the old cat by the scruff of her neck and trying to keep her face out of the water. It helped that I'd taken lifeguard training, lives ago on Long Island, and the Black Sea was warm that night with the whole, stored-up summer. I like to think that Princess trusted me too — or at least understood the man would have killed us.

After what felt like an hour, I rested for a while, floating on my back. Maybe I heard an engine muttering, far away; then I heard nothing. "We're safe," I told the wheezing, trembling cat, alone with me in the starless sea. I couldn't see my free hand in front of my face; I couldn't see Princess's eyes. "Don't be afraid. We'll just float here till the sun comes up. Which it will." She gave me a long, lamenting meow, as if she'd figured out there was no place to run, and she might as well stick it out with me.

Closing my eyes for a moment, I felt her small heart beating in the pit of my arm. Then above us I saw a pale gleam: a half moon, through the thinning fog.

MAYBE I DOZED a little; but if I let go of the cat

she clung to my bra, snuffling and sneezing now and then, to remind me she'd rather be sitting on her pillow.

"If we ever find dry land, I promise you a better pillow," I assured her, and she actually meowed. "Now can you lend me one of your extra lives?" I was beginning to feel awfully thirsty, and my empty stomach grumbled and groaned. The sea stayed smooth, or I couldn't have helped her keep her head out of the water.

Now I could clearly see the moon. Soon I saw stars, which raised my spirits; I saw the Big Dipper; I saw the North Star. Then suddenly Princess shook her head hard. In the thin light I saw her pricking up her ears.

"Hear something?" I couldn't, straining. Then I saw lights, and heard a purring that soon became a confident roar: the motor of a big, strong boat! Rapidly three white lights grew larger. How could anybody see us?

"Help!" I yelled in English. We had nothing to wave, to get attention. "Over here!" I screamed, treading water. I thought to pull Princess around my neck, so I could wave at the oncoming lights; but she stood up on my shoulder, dug her claws into my tangled hair and howled.

What a sight we must have made: I was dressed in a bra, and my hood was a cat near the end of one life. The patrol boat stopped its engine, and glided close, to get a better look.

I saw men in uniforms waving at us. They yelled something in Bulgarian, and a life preserver on a rope slammed into the water, yards away. Princess was all tangled in my hair, or I might have lost her then. With the last of my strength, with the cat on my head, I breast-stroked over to the floating ring, and those wonderful sailors hauled us in. They flung a net of ropes over the side of their boat, but I was too exhausted to climb up; so three of them clambered down together and dragged us out of the sea.

"Strange fish tonight," cried a voice in English. "A mermaid — with a cat!"

LATER I GOT to know the good-natured British naval officer who made that crack: on loan from NATO, he was advising the Bulgarian navy about intercepting people-smugglers. When Bulgaria joined the European Union, the Black Sea became another Rio Grande. Lucky for us that patrol was equipped with American night-vision gear.

The sailors found a life-preserver from the *Swoboda,* but not the boat — or Borislav. I hope he went to the bottom of the Black Sea, where he belongs. It's actually full of sulfuric acid.

I think Princess likes Long Island. She has a velvet pillow here. Old as she is, she's in excellent health, and may last many years, the vet says.

As for my tale about my grandma's life, I decided to write my own first.   🐾

Anna Sykora, aspiring scribe, lives in Hanover, Germany, with the world's most patient husband and three humongous Norwegian Forest Cats: Columbus, who eats with his foot; Dora, who drums on the windows and the bathtub every day; and Ellie, who nibbles away at the cacti, furnishings, computer cables, and window frames as if they were the gingerbread in "Hansel and Gretel." (Tales to follow.)

A CRY TO WAKE THE DEAD

Christine Sutton

LAPIS GAVE a disconsolate mew. He had not meant to cause any trouble. He'd only been trying to keep warm, and the frayed old mat in front of Mo's meagre fire had seemed the least cold spot in a room full of draughts and chills. Now Mo was lying on the sofa with her ankle swathed in bandages, while that interfering old fusspot from upstairs bustled about spouting all kinds of nonsense.

"He's got to go, Mrs Daley, he really has. Why, if I hadn't been passing your door and heard you go down you could have been lying there for who knows how long. I know he's company for you and all that; but, really, he's becoming a menace. And that meow of his is enough to wake the dead."

Mo shifted slightly on the threadbare sofa, trying to work her tiny frame into a more comfortable position.

"Oh, it wasn't Lapis's fault, Mr Malcolm," she said, stroking still shaky fingers across the heart-shaped head, "he doesn't understand about failing eyesight and stiff joints, do you, Lappy, dear? I couldn't part with him, we've been together far too long."

Mr Malcolm's face assumed a sour-lemons expression.

"An inch nearer to the hearth and you wouldn't

have been together any longer, though, would you, dear? *You'd* have been knocking on the pearly gates, while he'd be heading for pussycat purgatory."

He gave a sudden and dramatic shiver, setting his fleshy cheeks wobbling like just-set jelly.

"Brrr, it's like an ice-box in here. I'll put another lump on the fire, shall I?"

His hand was already delving in to the coalscuttle when Mo shook her head.

"No, please don't, Mr Malcolm. That bag's got to last me the whole weekend. Don't worry, I'll be right enough with this blanket and your nice cup of tea to warm me. And Lapis is as good as a hot water bottle, aren't you, darling?"

Lapis responded by marching up and down on his mistress's chest like a soldier on parade, studying his enemy with unblinking sapphire eyes.

"That thing hates me," said Mr Malcolm petulantly, tugging on his lower lip. "It's got a way of looking at me that's downright insolent."

"Lapis is a cat, Mr Malcolm," Mo said, pragmatic as always, "he doesn't know how to be insolent."

Mr Malcolm's sooty fingers had given him a rather fetching coal-dust goatee; and she bit back a smile, wondering whether she should mention it. Mischievously, she decided against it. It really rather suited him. The end of a broken spring was beginning to make its presence felt in her rear and she lifted her buttocks high to push it back down. As the heavy grey blanket began to slide to the floor Mr Malcolm hastened to retrieve it. He was tucking it back in when Lapis gave a sharp, mistrustful hiss.

"There, I told you. It hates me," he repeated, swiftly withdrawing his doughy fingers from the vicinity of the cat's flexed claws.

"Well, maybe you were mean to him in another life," Mo laughed, completely unperturbed.

Her neighbour gave a haughty sniff.

"Oh, so cats *can't* be insolent but they *can* be reincarnated?"

"Well, they do have nine lives," she reminded him with a twinkle in her eye.

A CRY TO WAKE THE DEAD

"Hmm," he muttered, unconvinced. "Well, it seems I've done all *I* can for you, Mrs Daley, so I'll leave you to the tender mercies of your pet. Think about what I said, though; or mark my words, he'll be the death of you."

As the door closed behind him, Mo lay back and let out a sigh. "Thank goodness for that," she said, snuggling under the blanket. "I know he means well; but, really, what an old woman." She sipped her tea and gently stroked the cat's silky head.

"Oh, you really are such a beautiful puss," she cooed over the rim of her cup. "Sometimes, when I look in those fabulous blue eyes of yours, I think I see glimpses of another world. What goes on behind them, hmm, Lappy? Have you got things all worked out, or is life as much of a mystery to you as it is to the rest of us?"

Lapis purred, the sound rattling in his throat like spring water over pebbles. If Mo was old by human standards then he was ancient, his markings no longer the rich, chocolaty brown they'd once been but more a muddy coffee colour, while his whiskers had as many grey patches as his mistress's hands had liver spots.

Little by little Mo's eyelids began to droop and the empty cup slid sideways on to the cushion. Lapis curled himself into a ball and settled down on her chest.

BUT WHILE Mo's slumber was the deep black pool of shock, Lapis's was filled with strange, disturbing images. He was in a room lit with glowing, golden light, where sumptuous draperies covered the walls; and the ceilings were supported by pillars lavish with gold leaf and encrusted with the lapis lazuli after which he'd been named. Yet for all the luxury of his surroundings, his ears and whiskers twitched as vague worries niggled at his mind.

AS THE FOG of sleep began to lift he became aware of a weird, high-pitched wailing sound that ebbed and flowed like distant waves. Curious, he started up to investigate. But before he could set so much as a paw on the cool marble floor, rough hands seized him by the scruff of the neck and threw him into a sack.

"You were ever the Queen's favourite," rasped a harsh voice in his ear, "time to ensure that you remain so for all eternity."

Desperately though Lapis fought to be free, the grip on the sack remained firm, the journey continued uninterrupted.

As the minutes passed he grew calmer, instinctively conserving energy for the moment when escape might finally become possible. For a brief while, the anguished wails grew louder and he sensed that his captor had taken to the city streets. Perhaps here he would get his chance. But all too soon they had faded to a far off keening, and the light filtering through the sack began to diminish.

The drop in temperature was sudden and dramatic, and Lapis knew he had reached journey's end. With a vicious shake the bag was upended, and he was cast unceremoniously on to the floor. As he emerged from its musty folds he saw his tormentor framed momentarily in the doorway. He caught a fleeting glimpse of the fleshy cheeks and tufted chin of Malkaii, the Queen's Chief Eunuch, before the huge sealing stone was rolled into place and the chamber fell horribly, ominously silent.

Terrified, Lapis threw himself across the room, blundering into golden statues and sending bowls and vessels skittering across the sandy floor. Chest heaving, he turned and saw the casket, gleaming dully in the light of four huge candles. One mighty leap and he was astride it, his claws scrabbling for purchase on the smoothly curving lid. Etched on top was the face of his mistress: the beautiful, doe-eyed Queen.

As the mocking echoes of his anguished wails filled the burial chamber, one by one the guttering candles went out. . . .

LAPIS WOKE with a start. The room was freezing, the fire long dead. He was perched on something stiff and unmoving. But it wasn't the casket. No, this was his beloved Mo and she was as cold as stone.

He nudged at her chin with his nose. No response. He rasped his tongue across her cheek. Her head lolled listlessly to one side. With mounting fear, he leaped on to the table and from there to the windowsill.

Pyramids of snow dotted the ledge, driven in through the cracks in the rotten wooden frame. He put his nose to the glass and let out a wail but there was no one out there this freezing cold night to hear. Jumping down, Lapis darted to the door. His memory was hazy, but it seemed to him that he had done all this before.

He hooked his claws in the gap and pulled hard. It moved just a fraction before sinking back into place. Desperately, he tried again. Crescents of milk-white nail sheared off at the base and embedded themselves in the wood, but the door remained stubbornly shut. Lapis sat back and let out the cry of a mortally wounded child.

Up in his bed, Mr Malcolm rolled over and looked at the clock. *Half three!* This was the last straw. No more excuses — that wretched cat just *had* to go. Wide awake now and furious as a pit full of rattle-snakes, he threw back the covers and reached for his robe.

DR HENRY THOMAS removed his glasses and thoughtfully wiped the snow from the lenses.

"It's lucky you found her when you did, Mr Malcolm," he said gravely, watching the stretcher disappear into the back of the ambulance, "she wouldn't have lasted the night. Shock can do funny things to a person, and in these temperatures . . ."

But Mr Malcolm shook his head.

"Wasn't me raised the alarm, Doc," he said, scooping up an elderly Siamese from the doorstep, "it was this old fellow. It's funny, I've often said his cry could wake the dead. Didn't think for one moment he'd take me seriously!" 🐾

Christine Sutton is a fifty-seven-year-old mum of one,

who lives with her partner Peter and twenty-year-old son Daniel in Hornchurch, Essex, about thirty minutes drive from London. She took up writing fifteen years ago after working for twenty-one years as a veterinary nurse.

Her work for adults and children has been widely published in magazines around the world, including Best, Yours, Progress, Woman's Own, Woman, Chat, Choice, The Lady, Candis, *and* Pet Magic *(all UK);* Fast Fiction *and* That's Life *(Australia);* Mum's Mag *and* Plus 50 *(S. Africa);* Dragonfly Spirit *(Canada);* Woman This Month *(Bahrain); and* Shades of Romance, Characters, Highlights, *and* Wee Ones *(America). She, Pete, and Daniel share their home with two dogs, Meggie and Gemma, and a long-haired tabby cat, Sophie.*

INVASION THWARTED

upon her pillow
where he put the mouse last week
he lays his trophies
green skin, a minute ray gun
she'll never guess he saved Earth

— Marcie Lynn Tentchoff

A CRY TO WAKE THE DEAD

ROMEO'S KISS

by Gabriel Beyers

THE PHONE RANG. Carol looked at her watch and sighed; five minutes before quitting time.

"Thank you for calling the Law Office of Haskins & Melview. This is Carol; how may I help you?" Carol's chipper tone belied her true feelings. On the phone a gruff-voiced man ranted for what seemed like ten minutes about a three-car pile-up that he caused, but wasn't his fault, no matter what the other drivers, the witnesses, or the cops said.

Carol thrust herself into the conversation as soon as the man took a breath. "I'm sorry sir, but Mr. Haskins and Mr. Melview have both gone home; and I'm afraid they won't be back until after New Year's."

The man wasn't happy.

Carol pulled her head-set off, resting it around her neck. The man's screaming continued.

Sara, the other receptionist, walked in from the next office. Sara was beautiful; tall with dark, corn-silk hair and green eyes. She had long, tan legs that made her mini-skirts seem all the more nonexistent.

That's good, Carol thought, *'cause she's as dumb as a bag of hammers.* A secret apology followed. Deep down Sara was a nice girl, and that made Carol want to spit on her so bad she could feel her mouth water.

Stop that.

She'll probably have a date every night between

Christmas and New Year's, and get over a dozen pro-posals before this time next year.

The man stopped screaming.

"Well, sir, I'm sorry we couldn't help you. If you'll just call back after the first of the year we will be glad to fit you in." The man hung up. Carol clicked on the answering machine.

Sara shook her head. "I'm so glad we've got the week off."

"Yeah, me too." A lie. Work seemed better than knocking around an empty house — especially on the holidays.

"Any big plans for Christmas and New Year's?"

Carol wanted to say no; to ask if she could tag along with Sara, but that was a level of pathetic she was un-willing to reach for — at least for now.

"Yeah, I've got a couple of parties lined up." Her self-loathing climbed another rung.

"That's great," Sara said. "Be extra careful. I heard another girl was raped last night."

"How awful," she said, her hand making an uncon-scious move to her mouth. "That's six in the past month."

"Scary, huh?"

"Is it the same guy?"

Sara shrugged her shoulders. "Police aren't releas-ing any information. Just that all the girls were at-tacked at home."

Carol's soul shriveled.

"Tomorrow's Christmas," Sara said. "People are supposed to be spreading good cheer and enjoying themselves, but instead we've gotta worry about some *crazy.*"

"Maybe we should walk out together."

"Yeah," Sara said. "Good idea. We should probably start doing that from now on."

Carol left work, but she couldn't bring herself to go home. Those poor girls, attacked in their own homes. Being raped is a horrible enough violation, but to have it happen in the place you feel the safest . . . abomina-tion.

SHE STOPPED at the little strip-mall close to Haskins & Melview. The sporting-goods store; she should be able to buy one there.

She tip-toed over the icy parking lot to the sidewalk. The wind gusted and a spray of snow from the top of a shoveled pile dusted her face. The cold sucked the breath from her and left her face feeling like a used pin cushion.

Damn it! Next year I'm going somewhere tropical for Christmas.

The heat from inside Fanatic Sports was a welcome friend. The store was a sea of sports bras and spandex shorts. Mountains of running shoes loomed in the distance. The hunting section was a forest of camouflage clothing. A rainbow of fishing tackle filled three aisles. A plastic deer stood grazing near a rack of orange vests.

Why would someone want to kill something as beautiful as a deer? Maybe a possum. Nothing but a giant rat. The thought of that long worm-like tail made Carol squirm. Yeah, she could shoot a possum.

The long glass cabinet showcasing handguns was hiding in the rear of the store. She bypassed the large guns — the ones she called *Dirty Harry* guns — and stopped at a tiny pistol that looked more cute than dangerous. What was it called? A Derringer?

She imagined herself with the little gun strapped to her inner thigh by a lace garter-belt. She didn't know why, but it made her feel sexy and powerful.

All that went away when she saw the price: two-hundred and fifty bucks.

"Can I help you ma'am?"

A man with an unkempt handlebar mustache and a shining bald head walked toward her. He had a bow-legged strut. He stroked his mustache with one hand while readjusting his crotch with the other. He leaned against the glass counter on his elbow, giving her an eye-groping while he sucked his teeth.

Carol stepped back. The man didn't seem to notice. She folded her arms across her chest, and his eyes sprang like a mousetrap to her face.

by Gabriel Beyers   113

"You lookin' ta buy a gun, are ya?" More teeth sucking.

"Oh, no . . . I was just looking." Was the dank cologne she was smelling right now the same that those six poor girls were still trying to wash off their skin?

"You just holler if you need somethin', okay sweetheart?"

Doors never seemed so inviting. Carol couldn't see him, but she just knew that nasty mustache-man was following her. Watching her.

OUTSIDE, the frigid air was even more ravenous. She wrapped her coat tight with her hands in the pockets. Another mist of snow slapped her in the face and she cursed out loud.

She flopped down in the seat of her Geo. Before she could close her door a tiny sound lifted from under her car.

Her heart fluttered. What was that? It sounded like a tiny voice saying *help*. She sat still, listening. Was it just the howling wind? The sound came again and this time she recognized it. It was a cat.

Carol bent down and looked under her car. Next to the far back tire, squatting like the great Sphinx, was a large Persian cat.

The cat's fur was smudged with dirt; tangled, except where large chunks seemed to be missing. A tattered feather-duster tail whipped around in agitation. Its head darted back and forth as if expecting an attack.

"Here kitty, kitty, kitty." The cat cringed. Its ears rolled like radar dishes. The poor thing didn't know where her voice was coming from. She continued to call.

The cat started to move. It staggered as if it couldn't determine which direction to go. Finally, it emerged from under the car.

Carol snatched up the cat. "It's a good thing I heard you. I might've run right over you, poor thing."

The cat surrendered in her arms, purring loudly enough to hear over the wind. Carol closed her door against the freezing winds. She examined the cat.

The cat's bulky size was nothing more than a disguise. A wire-frame skeleton hid just beneath the thick fur. The cat raised its head. Its eyes were large and round like marbles, white as the snow outside, and blind as both.

Carol swallowed a huge knot of pity. She couldn't just leave it here. The cat wouldn't survive the night. It didn't have a collar or I.D. tag around its neck. It must be a stray.

She started the car and cranked up the heat (which sputtered like a chain smoker running a marathon).

"I doubt the Vet is open on Christmas Eve," Carol said. "I'll take you home and we'll see if we can't get you in to see the doctor in a few days. Do you wanna come home with me?" The cat meowed as if to say yes. She couldn't help but smile.

A LONG driveway, marked by the tire tracks in the snow, led back to a tiny one-story house standing alone in a field. Clusters of trees stood round about, but not enough to disguise the emptiness. The surrounding houses, with their twinkling Christmas lights, were distant and seemed only figurines.

The house was lightly furnished: a matching green couch and love-seat; a couple of end-tables with lamps; a modest TV set in the corner; a simple bed and dresser in the bedroom. Nothing fancy.

Carol placed the cat on the couch. She threw her coat down on the arm of the love-seat. She placed her hand in front of the cat's nose so not to scare it when she sat down. The cat sniffed her hand, then licked her fingers.

In the house she had a better view of the cat. There were no injuries that she could see; just bald patches here and there. As she stroked the cat a large plug of fur came loose from its back.

"You poor baby," she said. "You've probably been around for a long time, haven't you? What should I call you? How about Princess? Do you like the name Princess?"

The cat rolled onto its back, legs spread, showing just why *Princess* was not the right name.

"Okay, Princess is out. How 'bout . . . Romeo?"

The cat rolled over and climbed into her lap. He made a couple of turns, flopped down, then released a continuous melody of rolling purrs.

"It's settled then. Romeo it is."

Carol put her head on the arm of the couch, kicked her legs up onto the cushions, all the while holding tight to Romeo. The remote control sat just out of her reach on the table above her head. Romeo climbed further up her body, now resting on her ribs, making it impossible to move without dumping him onto the floor.

It was 6:08 P.M. The wind outside howled, and the house hummed under its strength. Romeo's purring continued in equally spaced cycles. She felt her eyes go closed, but didn't realize they remained that way. Random thoughts poured down through the hourglass of her mind until it was empty. She could fight no longer. Sleep conquered.

THE DOORBELL rang.

A spray of hot, moist air caressed Carol's lips. She opened her eyes and was startled by two white orbs floating before her. Romeo was squatting on her chest, his tiny wet nose pressed to hers. The cat's weight seemed to have tripled. The milky blind eyes caused an involuntary gasp. Her throat closed and her lungs burned as they cried out for oxygen.

Carol sat up — sending Romeo tumbling onto her lap — and grabbed her throat. Her trachea opened as if she hit a release button, and a rush of cool air swept into her lungs. She began coughing, a little at first, then uncontrollably.

The doorbell rang again.

It was almost 7:00 according to the clock on the wall. Who in the world would be out here this late on Christmas Eve? She scooped Romeo into her arms, and went to the door. She pressed her ear to the door. The cold metal felt good on her hot face.

"Who is it?"

"It's Frank — your mailman."

Frank had been her mailman for over a year now, and was probably the nicest man she knew. She shifted Romeo into one arm, then opened the door with her free hand. Frank stepped inside, shivering like a wet dog.

Frank, although blessed with niceness, was not so lucky in the looks department. He was a short, heavy-set man with a balloon-animal look to him. His round face was shiny with oil, which made the pock marks all the more noticeable. He had a Cheshire smile — which isn't a bad thing, except for his heavy supply of rotten teeth. The synergy of the two was a little over-powering.

Frank scratched at the wiry black hair that was poking out from under his toboggan. "Is everything all right, Carol? I thought I heard you choking."

"I'm fine. I just got a little cat hair caught in my throat." She shifted Romeo back into both arms. Frank's eyes lit up like a child's, and Carol caught one of her many suspicions that Frank was a little slow.

"When did you get a cat?" Pure elation.

"Today, actually. I found him under my car." She hoisted the cat higher. "I named him Romeo."

Frank reached out, but before his gloved hand met fur, the cat's ears scissored back. He let out a low, roll-ing growl; then a hiss. Frank jerked his hand back.

"Romeo! I'm sorry about that, Frank. I forgot to tell you that he's blind. You must've scared him."

Frank flashed a smile of many colors. "Sorry 'bout that, Romeo." He looked the cat over, petting him with his eyes. "How old do you think he is?"

A silent sigh erupted in her mind. How long was she going to have to suffer Frank tonight? The record was over thirty minutes. It wasn't that she minded talking to Frank. She just felt a bit too tired tonight.

"He looks old," Frank said.

"I'm not sure. I'd say he's around fifteen."

"I don't think so. My mother had a cat — Spalding — that lived to twenty-three, and he looked better than this cat even after he was dead."

Carol forced a smile to keep from saying anything mean to poor, simple Frank the mailman. She didn't know why she took offense to what Frank said, but she did.

"Well, I'd say he's been wandering outside for a while. Maybe a little love will bring him around. So, how old do *you* think he is?"

"Every bit of twenty-five."

Twenty-three. Twenty-five. Who cares?

Frank flashed another brown-toothed smile. "At least he'll have a warm place to run out the clock."

She didn't like that image at all. She hadn't thought about that part, yet. Waking up, rolling over, and *Yuck!* there's a stiff cat stuck to your pillow. The skin on the back of her neck moved down six inches.

Frank shifted from side to side and flashed another smile that reminded her way too much of Indian corn.

She was so tired. Romeo squirmed in her arms as if to say, *stay if you want but I'm outta here.* It was time to be direct.

"Is there something you need, Frank?"

Frank's eyes widened a bit. "Oh, yeah. Sorry." He reached inside his blue jacket bearing the United States Postal Service emblem and pulled out a small stack of envelopes. "Here's your mail."

She shifted Romeo back into one arm and took her mail with her free hand. "Frank, you didn't need to bring my mail to the door. I could've walked out and got it."

Frank's round face wrinkled with a small embarrassed grin. "I was runnin' late today. When I got here I saw you was already home. I didn't want you to hafta get out in the snow and walk all that way to your mailbox. Especially with all the, y'know . . ." He leaned in and whispered the rest. ". . . rapes."

Her mouth soured, like she had a cheek-full of pennies. It was the way Frank said it more than anything. His eyes shifting side to side; a small grin on his face. He looked like a kid whispering a curse word to his friends.

Another forced smile. "Well, thank you, Frank. I appreciate it."

"You're welcome. Well, I better get going. Have a merry Christmas."

"You too, Frank."

"And you have a merry Christmas, too, Romeo." Frank tried again to pet Romeo, but the cat wouldn't have it. Romeo recoiled as if he could see Frank's approaching hand, hissed, then swatted with his paw.

"Romeo!"

"Oh, that's all right," Frank said. He smiled, but there was hurt swimming in his eyes. "No harm, no foul. I better get outta here. See ya later."

Carol shut the door; checked the locks, twice. She carried Romeo into the kitchen, placed him on the floor, then went to the refrigerator. Romeo squatted as if ready to run at any moment. He let out a small whimpering meow.

"I'm right here, Romeo." She grabbed the milk, then took a bowl from the cabinet. "I'm sorry but I don't have any cat food. Will milk be all right for a few days? I think I have some tuna in the pantry."

Another meow, this one higher, with a happy curl to it. She laughed. It was almost as if Romeo understood her.

She sat the bowl in front of Romeo, careful not to startle him. The cat lapped the milk with loud, fast strokes.

"Poor guy." She caressed Romeo's fur, which seemed cleaner, more full than before. "You probably haven't had any milk since you were a kitten, have you?"

In the pantry there were four cans of tuna left over from her *Atkins Diet* fiasco. She fed a can to the electric opener, drained the spring water into the sink, then dumped the meat onto a paper plate.

The cat sat next to the empty bowl, licking his mouth.

"That was fast."

Romeo didn't bother with an answer. He buried his muzzle into the tuna.

The room was tattooed with shadows. She turned on the rest of the lamps, chasing away the darkness, but the gloom remained. In the fireplace a white photo album was perched atop the pyramid of wood. On the mantel was a bronze cup filled with long matches.

Carol retrieved the book. FOREVER TOGETHER was written in gold lettering on the spine. It started with the wedding. Such a beautiful dress. How she had cried. Both of their families, all their friends. The perfect day. The album moved on: the house — five bedrooms, three and a half baths, the cars . . . the happiness. It was odd how one-sided photo albums were. All good memories and not a trace of bad. No pictures of him and his whore. No laminated Divorce Decrees. No receipts for money paid to blood-sucking lawyers (all too similar to the leeches she worked for). Photo albums were denial in the flesh.

She placed the album in its spot as ice-peak of the wooden mountain. She took a match from the bronze cup, struck it, watched it burn. Black threads defied gravity, reaching for the ceiling. The flame danced in the throes of passion. She pushed the match toward the wood — toward her memories. She was really going to do it this time. Time to move on. But if the memories were gone, what was left?

The dancing flame perished in one blow. The stick, with its point of charcoal, joined the pile of its friends next to the wood.

The rest of the night was spent confined to the couch by a mass of purring fur. It wasn't a problem, though. At least this Christmas Eve wouldn't be spent alone.

CHRISTMAS Eve clicked into the early part of Christmas Day. Carol pushed the power button on the remote control and the TV sizzled into blackness. She carried Romeo to her bedroom. Romeo growled (a tiny one) when she placed him on the bed, then looked up with his white eyes.

"I'm sorry. I have to change clothes."

Frank's words came rolling back: *a place to run out the clock*. The thought of Romeo lying next to her face, stiff and dead, brought a case of the shivers. But what to do? Romeo sat bathing his crotch, one rear leg pressed straight up. He seemed in all right shape, even if he was in his twenties. She'd have to chance it.

She stripped down to her bra and panties before she

realized the curtains were open. An overpowering sense of vulnerability hit her. The thought of watching eyes hiding in the darkness outside produced the sensation of something cold and slimy coiling around her legs.

She reached for her robe, all the while keeping her eyes fixed on the window. With her nakedness buried in a cocoon of cotton, she ventured over to the window. From a safe distance there was nothing but a transparent reflection; an apparition with black eyes. Closer she could see the glow of moonlit snow. Closer. The apparition vanished, replaced by a circle of breath-fog. The tree clusters stood as dark giants in the distance.

But what about under the window, where you couldn't see? How strong was this glass? Could someone really reach though and grab you like in the movies?

Carol backed away. On the upper pane of the window, wiped into a patch of frost, were four parallel smears. Almost as if four fingers —

Carol pulled the string and the blinds dropped with a heavy *whoosh*. She backed away from the window until the bed hit the back of her legs. She told herself it was her own fingers that had left the marks; that she missed that spot on the window last fall. It wouldn't help her sleep, but it might keep her eyes from being glued to the window.

The robe came off just long enough to trade in her bra for a T-shirt and a pair of thick cotton pajama-pants. Romeo was curled into a ball, sleeping. She climbed into bed.

She fished the remote control out from under her pillow and turned on the TV. *It's a Wonderful Life.* She wasn't in the mood for black-and-white right now. *A Christmas Story* was on a few channels down. It was almost over — the part where Ralphie almost shoots his eye out — but it was playing on a continuous loop for twenty-four hours, so she'd just catch it again.

Carol left the bedside lamp turned on. Being in the dark didn't seem like such a good idea right now.

She didn't make it to the end of the next showing.

Her eyes grew heavy about the time Ralphie's friend, Flick, was learning a valuable lesson about why a frozen flagpole and your tongue should never meet. By the time the school-yard fight scene rolled around she was asleep.

Carol drifted in and out of muddy, half-developed dreams.

RUNNING across a frozen desert. Splinters of emotions: sadness; a sense of being unique; a smothering loneliness.

People were chasing her. Fierce. Bloated on hate. She couldn't see them. She just knew they were there. They were always *there.*

The desert crumbled into pieces and scattered like a fleeing shoal of fish. Colors blended like blood mixing in water.

A room made of giant stone blocks. A man stood in the shadows. So young, so beautiful. His bronzed face was kind and gentle.

Jewels spilled from the beautiful man's hands. A gift.

Something was wrong. The jewels became grave-bugs, scattering across the floor. The kind man's skin grayed; he fell in a heap. A death wound opened in the back of his skull.

Pain ripped Carol from her dream. Her blood solidified into ice. Her throat closed. Her brain tried to escape through the eye sockets. Romeo was sitting on her chest, his mouth pressed to hers. She opened her mouth, trying to steal some air, but her lungs were no longer there. Nothing but fire exploding beneath her breasts.

She looked up into white eyes surrounded by brown fur. She arched her back, dislodging Romeo. The cat made a nonchalant leap onto the pillow beside her head and sat there as if awaiting a treat.

Her mind funneled back down into her body, then the lungs opened. The first draught of breath felt coarse and dirty. It came in like smoke, and forced its way back out just the same.

Carol burst into a coughing fit.

Romeo sat on the pillow, waiting patiently. The choking dwindled and she was reduced to scattered, short breaths. She tried to clear her throat, but it only brought up a small vomit of stomach acid.

"That's twice, you little —" Another cough rose, cutting her words short. "Twice," she continued, "that you've almost choked me to death in my sleep. Are you *trying* to kill me?"

Romeo responded by cleaning his chest.

She struggled to hold onto her little dagger of anger, but the old cat's indifference was defeating her. Cats always seem so calm, as if they designed the world and knew all of its secret workings. Romeo's attention to his hygiene was his way of saying: *I knew you'd be all right.*

Romeo finished his primping, let out a small meow, then crawled, purring, into her lap. The fight was over. Feline: 1, human: 0.

She crossed her legs Indian-style and Romeo nestled into the pocket. She stroked the cat's coat with both hands, forcing her finger through the thick fur. Something was different.

Romeo seemed a little thicker than he had earlier. His tiny frame of toothpick-bones was now hidden under a plump layer of muscle. The old cat's fur didn't seem as patchy as before, either. She ran her hands down the cat's body, half petting, half searching. Romeo didn't seem to care which. His body lengthened beyond its limit as he yielded to an involuntary stretch.

She couldn't be sure. Maybe Romeo's fur really wasn't *that* patchy. It was cold when she found him; she was in a hurry to get home. Maybe he looked worse than he was. All the cat needed was a little food and a warm place to rest.

Romeo looked up. Two narrow pupils floated beneath the thin milky sheen. She leaned in for a better look, but the old cat wasn't much for second chances. He made an arching jump from her lap and trotted out of the bedroom.

Carol stood up and wrapped her robe tight. She started for the bathroom but a sudden dizziness swept her backwards.

There was a weakness she had never felt before,

like something had sucked the marrow from her bones. She felt thin — not in terms of her weight, but in her presence in the living world. Her skin was made of tissue paper that could be defiled and destroyed with the slightest touch.

It took some effort, but she stood to her feet. Her legs wobbled like strands of tie-wire. Somehow she stayed vertical. She took a few steps, her knees buckling in and out. The thought of newborn ponies popped into her head, and she laughed without meaning to. Her legs caught a drink of strength. After a few moments her knees no longer knocked around. A tingling remained in her calves and thighs, and her ankles felt swollen, but she was miles above where she had been.

She walked into the bathroom. In the mirror stood a pale, gaunt replica of herself. Should she call a doctor? Could she even get a doctor on Christmas? The emergency room would be open.

She decided a hot shower would do her more good than any doctor could.

GETTING DRESSED was more of a chore than anticipated. Simple movements stole her breath, and she had to stop and rest between each layer. She sat on the edge of the bed fighting the desire to jump back under the covers.

Where's that cat, she wondered. A long curling meow came from the living room as if the old cat had picked the thought out of the ether.

"Romeo, sweetheart, you okay?"

Romeo answered with another meow, this one with a little more growling distress. He was sitting next to the front door. His calls grew louder and more desperate as she approached.

"What's wrong, Romeo?"

The old Persian stood on his hind legs and pressed his marbled front paws to the door.

"Damn cat, you've gotta quit that," she said with a laugh. "You're creeping me out a little." Romeo turned his milky eyes toward her. She wasn't sure why, but she said, "Sorry, just kiddin'."

She grabbed her thick wool trench-coat and a pair

of snow boots (the kind that slipped on rather than tied, and was stuffed full of faux-fur) from the hall closet. Romeo fired off another round of cries.

"I'm hurrying, I swear to God. Cut me some slack. I appreciate you letting me know you have to crap, but I feel like I'm ten seconds away from barfing."

Romeo stopped meowing.

The boots were soft, spongy lead weights; the trench coat was cumbersome. The more she moved, the more frustrated she got. The frigid air pinched her cheeks as soon as she cracked the door. Her breath shot out in a horizontal geyser.

Romeo bolted through the small crack in the door. He crossed the small porch in a bounce, then disappeared behind the snow-covered bushes that ran along the front of the house.

"Hey, you little fart, get back here." She stepped onto the porch, shutting the door behind her. "Don't forget you're blind," she shouted. "I'm not chasing after you if you get lost."

SHE COUNTED to ten in her head, then went chasing after the cat.

The snow was deep and miry. It stuck to her boots like wet clay, adding weight to each step. She stopped every few steps to bend over and peer under the bushes. No Romeo. At the end of the bushes was a patch of yellow snow and a pile of turds covered by a quick dusting of snow (cats do love to hide their business). Paw prints in the snow led around the corner of the house.

The wind gusted and she stumbled in a deep drift. She stayed standing — just barely though. Should she go on? What if she did fall? She felt too weak to get back up.

Her ankles were wet and stinging. She hadn't planned on a hike through Winter Wonderland and now her boots were full to the brim with snow.

The surrounding houses were mere bumps on the horizon. In the beginning the privacy seemed nice; no one close enough to spy or press themselves into her business. Now she felt stranded. If she fell and couldn't get up, the chances were slim to none that anyone would notice her. She would just lie out here in this tundra until she froze to death. All for a cat that would probably be dead in a few days anyhow.

"Romeo. Here kitty, kitty, kitty." She tried to mask her desperation to the cat, but wasn't sure why.

The wind was already laying waste to the trail she'd cut in the snow. *Go back in,* she told herself, *Romeo will find his way back to the front door.* But what if he didn't? There was no way the old cat had enough fight in him to last the night.

She turned the corner and saw Romeo near the back of the house. She called for him, but the cat didn't stir. He stood hunkered down in the middle of a patch of flattened snow.

She waded through the snow, which was now above her knees. Her teeth chattered loud enough to deafen. She called to Romeo every couple of steps in hopes that he wouldn't become alarmed and delve deeper into the snow. He didn't. When she made it to him, the cat turned and looked up. Then she saw what had been keeping the old cat's attention.

Romeo stood with his front paws on top of a large crow. A dead crow. The bird's head was tilted sideways and one milky-white eye stared up at the heavens as if expecting to see its comrades coming to its rescue. The black feathers contrasted with the snow so much that it seemed more like a hole piercing the ground than a three dimensional creature.

"Romeo, did you —" She stopped herself. There was no way. Romeo's eyes were as milky-white blind as that dead bird's. Even if the old cat was a zen-master with his other four senses, there was no way he could've crept up on that crow.

She knelt down to get a closer look at the bird. There wasn't any blood. Cat-attacked birds always had puncture wounds somewhere, either by claw or fang. This crow didn't look harmed at all — just dead. Its feathers were all ragged and loose. Just like her parakeet, Rosco, when she was ten. Rosco looked like that, all loose and frazzled, right before he died. Old birds just looked like that. Like an overused feather duster.

That's what it was. Romeo wasn't a bird murderer — at least not this time. It was Father Time that stole this bird's glory. Still, though, the small circle of packed snow did make it look like there had been a struggle. And was that a small trail of steam lifting out of the crow's open mouth?

No. She banished the thought. The crow died sometime earlier and Romeo just smelled his way over here. She scooped Romeo up around the mid-section, careful not to touch the dead crow.

The sun peeked from behind the clouds. She looked up, and that's when she noticed the thin trail in the snow that connected her bedroom window to some distant point.

"You've gotta be kidding me!"

She pushed through another drift to get to the trail. Though the wind had dusted it over with fresh snow, there was still no mistaking what had formed it. Boot prints — some coming, some going — embedded in the snow like fossils in a rock. She remembered the window. The finger marks on the glass.

Tears welled up, turned cold, and threatened to freeze. Carol scanned the open field. Maybe it was just a neighbor boy hoping to catch a peep. But what if it wasn't? What if it was the . . . *rapist?* He could jump out at any moment — could come running across the yard, truth be told — and there would be no hope of making it back inside. She was too weak. Too thin.

Romeo hissed and she flinched so hard that she almost dropped him in the snow.

"W-what's w-wrong R-R-Romeo?" She didn't know anymore if it was the cold or just flat-out fear that was turning her into a chattering, shivering mess.

Romeo hissed again.

She spun around twice, almost in hysterics. Nothing. Nothing but Old Man Winter.

She had to get back inside, and now. Any longer and she was going to end up like that crow. The rapist or the cold. One of them was going to get her. It didn't matter which. She was too frail right now to defend herself against either.

Backtracking the trail she'd cut in the snow proved no easier. Her legs were quivering pillars of burning lava surrounded somehow by a shell of icy numbness. With every step the snow collapsed in around her feet and held fast like concrete. She kept turning around, sure that some long-haired, foul smelling creature would be closing in on her. No one was. Still, when she faced forward, she could feel his red-rimmed eyes groping after her.

Carol all but fell through the front door. Romeo growled a bit as she fumbled between him and the locks. She kicked off her boots, splashing snow and slush in all directions. She removed her wet socks by stepping on the toes and pulling, all the while trying not to drop the old cat.

Romeo squirmed with discomfort, so she deposited him on the couch. He sat with his massive tail wrapped around and across his front paws. A pose worthy of a statue. He watched her, following her with his blind gaze, as she hopped out of her wet jeans.

Carol cocooned herself over one of the registers with a quilt her grandmother had made. The hot air caressed her, and the remaining cold bled from her flesh. She clicked on the TV, but before she could get interested in anything, weariness took hold. She fell asleep, head bobbing between her knees.

WHEN SHE woke up the sun had pulled in its golden blanket. The house was dark except for the light vomiting from the TV.

A large message, written in red, flashed across the top right corner of the screen: **BREAKING NEWS**. She caught the anchorwoman's voice in spurts.

". . . unidentified woman . . . found dead . . . raped . . . same M.O. . . . . mutilated . . ."

Carol stayed awake the rest of the night, but not by choice. Every bump, every creak of the house, every gust of wind sent her into a seizure of panic. The wind was laughing at her. It enjoyed twisting the house until the wooden frame groaned, just so it could watch her scurry around like a rabbit trapped in a dog pen.

In the drawer next to the kitchen sink, way in the

back, was a ring box. It was under some old papers as if it were a lost and forgotten thing. But it wasn't. She didn't sell her wedding ring after Mike left her. That's just what she told everyone. She slipped it on. It still fit. Still sparkled. Still made her feel better when she was scared and alone. Almost like Mike was still there.

It wasn't until the sun returned, pushing its way through the curtains, that she drifted off to sleep.

THE DESERT SAND burned her feet. Voices from behind. Shouts of hatred. They killed him; the dark-skinned man. Because of her.

She slipped and fell. Her face pounded into unyielding grit. She couldn't get up. Too weary. Too thin. The sand crawled upward into her mouth like billions of fire-winged gnats. The sand packed her throat. It climbed into her sinus. She felt her cheeks expand to the point of splitting. Her lungs became an hourglass — filling, burning — marking her end.

She knew Romeo was sitting on her chest before she even opened her eyes. His paws were kneading her breast like dough. His cold nose pressed against her upper lip.

She sat up, arms flailing, feet kicking. Romeo jumped off and landed on the back of the couch. She tried to take a breath but her lungs were gone. All that remained were the two familiar sacks of fire smoldering beneath her ribs. She gagged. Her stomach wrenched tight, and her esophagus felt as though a Great Dane was squeezing his way up. She thought she was going to vomit. The gun fired, but it was out of ammo. Instead, a burning spurt of bile hit the roof of her mouth, followed by a symphony of involuntary swallowing.

A flash-flood of rage, she turned to the old cat with the intention of grabbing him and practicing her softball pitch. Romeo sat on the back of the couch, posing like the Great Sphinx, eyes half closed. The anger vanished in such a hurry that it left a vacuum in her soul.

Romeo released a small purring meow, as if he knew the havoc he was playing with her emotions. She laughed (just a small one; her throat still felt tight and raw) and cupped the cat's head in both her hands, scratching his cheeks. She kissed Romeo on the top of his head.

"Are you hungry, baby?"

She grabbed a can of tuna from the cabinet. The words on the label were blurry. Great! Not only fat and wrinkles, but now glasses.

There was a thud as Romeo landed on the floor. The click-clack of his nails on the linoleum could be heard even over the can-opener. Carol scraped the fish, spring-water and all, into a small bowl. The smell was overpowering. She dropped the bowl in front of Romeo.

Another nap, she thought, *that's what I need.* She was on the couch, getting ready to tumble onto her side when Romeo sent up a shrill call. She stopped in mid-fall. She wanted to scream, but instead she just sighed.

Romeo sat by the front door, scratching at the threshold.

"I can't let you out," she said, almost begging. "I'm too sick to stay out there with you."

Romeo meowed.

"I know you have to take a dump, but you could get lost. Just go in the bathtub."

Another meow, this one soft — desperate.

"Fine." Romeo drifted over to the side, allowing her room to open the door. "If you get lost, then tough. I ain't comin' out to find you." But she knew Romeo wouldn't get lost. The way she knew he could find his way around without so much as a stumble. The way she knew the cat could understand her, as if he were once human. The way she knew she loved him, desperately needed him, and truth be told, would brave the terrible snow, soaking wet and buck-naked, just to find him.

"Just scratch the door when you want back in. I'll be listening." Something rose in her heart, and she blurted it out before she was able to evaluate it. "Please come back." Hearing the words hit the air brought both a shudder and a release.

Romeo rubbed against her legs.

"I promise I'll go to town later and buy you a litter box so you won't have to go out. I just need a little more time to rest. Let the after-Christmas crowds die down."

Winter reached in the open door and punched her. Once again she felt her existence go thin. Romeo trotted out into the snow as it if were a field of whipped cream. He disappeared behind the bushes.

What if she fell asleep again? What if she couldn't hear Romeo's scratches?

Carol left the door open just a crack. Enough so that the old cat could push it open if he wanted. It wouldn't be a problem for Romeo.

The next time she did this little trick, it wouldn't be Romeo that found his way inside.

A COLD BLAST hit her feet and crawled up her legs. She sat up on the couch with a start. Had she been asleep? She didn't know.

The clock on the wall was blurry. She rubbed her eyes and looked again. None better.

A ball of fur darted across the living room floor and disappeared into the bedroom. She screamed and pulled her feet off the floor before she realized who it was.

She went to the front door, closed and locked it. "That's it. I'm going right now to buy you a litter box. To hell with the after-Christmas crowds."

CAROL had hoped that by the time she was cleaned up and dressed her vision would come around. It didn't. She finally gave up and walked over to the clock in her bedroom. Two-thirty in the afternoon, and she was already exhausted enough to pass out. The bed was calling to her. *No! No more letting Romeo out to roam.* The cat needed a litter box and some normal cat food. No more milk and tuna.

Romeo refused to come out from under her bed, no matter how hard she coaxed. All she wanted was to kiss him goodbye. He knew that. Why was he acting this way?

The old cat nestled in the far corner — the darkest corner. He turned his head, and his eyes flamed green with reflected light; the animal eye-shine outlined the slitted pupils hidden beneath the cataracts.

"Fine!" Carol said. She climbed to her feet. She started to leave the room, but stopped at the door. Not sure why, she said, "I love you."

A meow.

That one little meow meant more than any of the gifts the men in her life had given her. It's amazing that an old cat could lift the weight of loneliness like no human could. It was like finding the man of her dreams, her soul-mate, her —

The title *Crazy Cat Lady* prevented her from pursuing this course of thinking any further.

CAROL stopped halfway to her Geo. Something black was sitting on top of the snow ten yards out. Another black *something* stood fifteen yards past that.

Carol squinted against the sun-charged snow. She couldn't see them clearly, but she knew what they were. Two more dead crows. Murdered by Romeo. But exactly how, she wasn't sure. Maybe the old cat wasn't blind after all. Is there such a thing as having albino eyes?

There was something past the second crow. A furry *something*. A rabbit, or maybe another cat; she couldn't tell. She wanted to wait and see if the furry thing moved, but the cold got the better of her.

She got in the car. The engine turned over with a lethargic grumble. The heat sputtered and choked. The air spilling forth was hardly warmer than outside.

Carol stared at the furry thing as the wind and snow conspired to bury it. *Had to be a rabbit,* she thought. *Not another cat. Romeo's too old. Even if he could — why would he?*

THE CLOSEST spot in the Pet Stop parking lot was three rows back. Even the pet store was having an after-Christmas rush. What little bit of energy the car heater bestowed upon Carol, the wind ripped away on her journey to the store. But it was the crowd that sent her meter plummeting to absolute zero.

Shoulder to shoulder. No air. People walking dogs.

Puddles and piles everywhere. *Morons!* Can't believe this. Hey, watch it! Merry Christmas to you, too. That bag of food looks too heavy. Maybe just a small one, and the litter box. Come back some other time. Too tired. Too thin. Can't breathe.

"Hello, how are you today?" asked the young man at the register.

Carol would have unloaded on him — in the true spirit of Ebenezer Scrooge — with every four-letter word she knew had he not been so handsome. Instead, she just smiled and said, "Fine, thanks."

The cashier was tall with dark hair; late twenties maybe. Not exactly a runway model, but those cobalt eyes with that chiseled chin sure got the job done. The cashier made small talk — mostly questions about Romeo — as he rang up the food and the litter box. Carol replied with short answers, feeling all the while that she was staring at him too long.

She didn't feel well. She knew she didn't *look* well, either. Would it have killed her to have done her hair, put on some makeup, something? He was too young anyway.

She handed over her credit card. Her eyes locked with those beautiful blue orbs for a brief moment. Her heart played xylophone on her rib cage. He flashed her a small broken smile, handed her the receipt, then looked away at the growing line.

Carol felt a little deflated. She signed the receipt, then turned to go.

"Excuse me, Miss."

Miss, not Ma'am, Carol thought. *It's not much, but it's a start.*

She wanted to say something witty; something sexy and alluring. Instead, she raised her eyebrows, looked expectantly toward the cashier, and grunted.

"There's a rebate on that litter box," he said. Carol deflated even more. "I'm out of slips to give you, but if you want to write down your name and address, I can make sure they mail you one."

He handed her a pen and piece of notebook paper. She scribbled down her information, hoping it was legible (since she couldn't read it herself).

The cashier looked it over. She thought another smile flashed across his face. Maybe he noticed that she wrote down her phone number, too — just in case. More likely, he was just repressing a laugh.

Carol felt the urge to explain herself. She opened her mouth, changed her mind, then turned and left the store without a backward glance.

She was home before she realized what she had forgotten. No kitty litter. A lot of good the box is going to do without the litter. She went inside and tossed the litter box and cat food on the kitchen counter.

"Sorry Romeo," she called out, "I screwed up. Looks like you'll have to dump in the snow until tomorrow. Too tired to go back out now."

It was on the floor — a large runny pile — over by the edge of the couch. She smelled it almost before she saw it. Romeo didn't have chance to make it to the snow.

CAROL was able to remove the stain, but the smell still lingered. She decorated the living room with every scented candle she owned. A large Christmas-cookie scented candle (the biggest one she had) was placed on the table next to the couch.

Carol fell face down on the couch and pulled her arms underneath her chest. She was starting to drift off when she was pulled back to reality by Romeo.

The old cat was meowing — a lot. She knew without even looking that he was at the front door. For a moment she considered ignoring the cat, but the thought of cleaning up another pile gave her the strength to sit up. She cursed herself under her breath. She just *had* to forget the kitty litter, didn't she!

Romeo added a chorus of door-scratching to his song.

"Be careful," she called out as the cat darted behind the bushes. She left the door cracked like before, then waddled back to the couch to give her waking mind back to the cushions.

CAROL woke with an instant sense of alarm, though what was causing her panic, she wasn't sure. Dusk had crept in, and the house was dark except for the spirited dancing of candle flames. She sat up and shivered. The room was saturated with cold. The front door was wide open.

A hole of insecurity opened in her chest, taking into itself all the heat that remained in her body. Carol stood up. Someone was outside. They were walking — no, running — toward the house.

Carol's legs turned to a stack of water-balloons. She made a weak-kneed dash for the door. The figure outside must have seen her because he picked up his pace. She grabbed the door and fell against it. It glided on its hinges, but before it could snap shut, a large arm came shooting inside to block.

The arm reached around like a striking snake and latched onto Carol's wrist with its meaty hand. She screamed and beat on the arm, but the hand held fast. She sank her teeth into the salty flesh near the thumb. A blast of warm blood filled her mouth. The man screamed and released his grip, but the bulky arm remained a wedge in the door.

The man threw his weight into the door. It burst open, catapulting Carol backward. The massive silhouette stepped inside, reached over to the wall, and flipped on the lights.

It was Frank the mailman.

Carol scuttled away. Frank just stood his ground. He seemed not to notice her at all, but instead, glared around the room with menacing hate. Then Frank ran at her in a half-crouched stance, never for a moment looking directly at her.

Carol rolled over onto her hands and knees. Frank snatched her by the ankles and pulled her towards him. Her legs kicked in all directions; her arms paddled as though swimming. But all the fighting and churning wasn't enough to free her.

Frank reached down, shoving his plump hands (one of them oozing blood) under Carol's armpits. He squeezed her hard around her upper ribs. Her lungs surrendered the small bit of air they held. The ground fell away as Frank lifted her without so much as a grunt. She thrashed like a netted fish and caught

Frank in the eye with her elbow. He released his suffocating grip, dropping her on her feet. She tried to run but he grabbed her by the shoulders.

Her legs were almost too flimsy to support her weight. Her breathing was broken and uncontrolled. Swirls of light danced on her eyes. She was going to faint. "Frank," she screamed. "No, please! Please don't!"

Frank spun her so that she faced him. He shook her so hard that her teeth clanged together like novelty dentures.

"Carol, someone's in the house!" Frank's voice was panicked and shaky. Carol just stared at him; her mind trying to fit the words together. He had a strange little grimace that just hinted at the Indian-corn teeth buried beneath his lips. "Did you hear me? Someone's in this house. I was delivering the mail. I saw a man sneak in the front —"

Frank gasped. Before Carol could turn to look, a blast of hot pain wrapped around the back of her head. The room filled with white star-bursts, each one collapsing into black holes.

Carol fell face down on the floor. Fire poured from the back of her head, down her spine and pooled in her thighs. She couldn't open her eyes or unclench her teeth. Her ears were ringing, but through that she could hear what she thought was thunder.

She turned onto her stomach and pushed herself up with the help of the wall. She stood on her knees. Shards from the lamp that was used to hit her head pierced her shins. She forced her eyes open. Everything was tinted red. She touched the back of her head, rekindling the lava of pain. She looked at the blood that covered her hands, felt it running down the back of her neck. She thought of the beautiful dark man in her dreams,

[*a death-hole opened in the back of his head.*]

then vomited.
The thunder grew louder, mixed with harsh voices.
Frank and someone else wrestled around the room.

　　　　　　　　　　　　　　　　　　ROMEO'S KISS

They seemed choppy and slow, as if caught in a strobe light. They twisted unnaturally clockwise, then counter-clockwise.

Carol closed her eyes and felt the vertigo ease.

The two men were stomping around in her belongings like crazed dancers. Frank, who had more weight to him, threw his attacker into the side table. The table jumped into the air like an electrocuted rabbit, hit the wall and dumped the large Christmas-cookie candle into the curtains.

The curtains went up like old newspaper.

The fire grew, but Carol was too tired — too thin — to stand and run. All she could do was watch with numb apathy.

Frank fell to his back with the other man on top of him. The attacker's dark hair glistened in the light of the fire that now consumed one whole wall. The man raised both hands above his head. He held a knife.

The knife shimmered like water in the sun for a moment, then disappeared into Frank-the-mailman's throat. Frank gave a loud gurgling shout. His arms and legs flailed violently, then he was dead.

The man pulled the knife out of Frank's throat, then turned his cobalt-blue eyes on Carol.

She knew this guy, but from where? The vertigo was returning. She leaned against the wall, but didn't realize it. She'd given this blue-eyed devil her address; had secretly wanted him to come. She forgot the litter; bought the box, but no litter. A rebate.

The young cashier dismounted Frank's corpse like a steed. The fire rippled across the ceiling. It wrapped itself around to the next wall. Carol felt the heat on her face. The light hurt her eyes. She turned and stumbled toward the front door. The cashier tackled her.

The cashier forced Carol to her back. He tore open her pants with greedy delight. She let out a broken, raspy scream. She tried to claw at his face, but every time she raised her hands he slashed at them with his knife. Exhausted, she dropped her arms. The blood gushed. He cut open her shirt.

Carol turned her head to the side. She was going to die. She knew it. She didn't want to see his horrible grin, smell his breath, look into those beautiful cobalt orbs of evil. She looked out the front door at the snow falling.

And there he was.

Romeo stood in the doorway, hissing. But something was different. There was a power about him. An authority. And in the firelight, she saw it.

His eyes! No longer milky-white. No longer blind. Now a brilliant green, each with a black slitted pupil shining like a jewel.

The cashier, ignoring Romeo, continued carving on Carol.

Romeo jumped at the man and latched onto his arm. The old cat climbed the cashier's shoulder like a tree branch, and he arched his back in pain. He slashed at Romeo with his knife, but the cat landed the first blow.

Romeo jumped off, leaving the cashier with a set of deep scratches across his left eye. The man tried to return the favor but Romeo darted out of reach.

Blood poured down the cashier's face. His upper eyelid was split into three pieces. He touched his eye, then howled.

The cashier stood up. "I'm going to feed you to the fire, you little shit!"

Carol moved for the front door with a primal lust for life. The cashier kicked her in the ribs hard enough to flip her onto her back again.

The cashier turned toward Romeo, then stumbled a little, as if drunk. His blue eye (the one not hidden behind a shredded lid) rolled upward, leaving only the white visible. He dropped his knife, and it fell to the floor with a clang. He stumbled to his knees, choking and gagging. He clawed at the scratches on his face; at the shredded eyelid. Then he went limp and fell onto his back.

Romeo climbed onto the cashier's chest. He pressed his muzzle to the man's lips. The cashier twitched, attempting to turn his head, but couldn't.

A soft hum reverberated around the room. Not

a noise. A presence. The rolling flames fled away from the cat. A star of light appeared in the cashier's mouth. The light pulsated and flooded upward into Romeo. The cashier's youthful body began to wither and turn gray. His dark hair whitened; his skin wrinkled like a deflated balloon. His blue eyes, wide with fear, fogged over until they were white marbles.

At first Carol thought the old cat was shrinking. His body fluttered, then collapsed, over and over. The light from the cashier's mouth swirled around the cat, growing brighter each time, until it was too brilliant to hold.

A moment of thunder-less lightning, then the fire-light regained control.

Carol opened her eyes. A small kitten, maybe only a few weeks old, sat on the dried-up corpse

[*My God! He looks a thousand years dead!*]

of the cashier. The kitten stared at her with luminous green eyes.

Romeo hopped from the snarling mummy and pranced up to Carol.

Fear blistered inside her. It had been Romeo's kiss that had left her so *thin*. What would he do to keep his secret? She tried to roll away but Romeo jumped onto her chest, pinning her down with an unnatural weight. He sat on her throat, smelling her face. She began to cry.

Romeo pressed his muzzle to her mouth. The burning house dissolved into the desert.

THE PEOPLE chanting. The beautiful dark man. Their king. Forever young, forever to rule. Those who sought to steal the King's magic. Murderers. The King's wounded head. No life left. Too late to give.

The flames reappeared.

Romeo, no longer a kitten, but now a young cat, sat on Carol's stomach. There was new strength in her body. The wounds on her hands and chest were gone. Only her blood-stained clothes remained as a witness to her struggle.

Carol wrapped her arms around Romeo, stood up and burst from the inferno like a newborn Phoenix.

SARA the receptionist stopped Carol in the hallway. "What have you done to yourself?" She circled, eying Carol with awe. "You look ten years younger."

Ten years was a good guess. Carol wasn't sure of the exact number, but judging from the way she felt, and looked, she thought ten years was a right good guess.

Carol went home to her rented apartment and was greeted at the door by Romeo. She fed him a can of tuna and a bowl of milk, then carried him to the couch. She sat stroking the cat's fur as he purred against her stomach.

Carol was thinking. There were a lot of things on her mind ever since her house, her possessions — her *old* life — went up in smoke and flames. Romeo could have drained the life from her anytime he wanted. But he only took tiny bits. Little drinks, just to stay alive. Romeo had not only saved the life she had, he had given her a little extra in return.

There were so many questions.

THOUSANDS of years had passed since the death of the beautiful king — she knew it the way she knew the sky is blue. No doubt countless, between then and now, had met the same end as that blue-eyed devil. But just the same, there *had* to have been others like her, right? Ones that showed mercy and were dealt mercy. If so, what of *their* end? Did they ask the same question she wanted to ask? If so, and Romeo agreed, where were they now? Why weren't they with him? Maybe Romeo said no, and turned again to the wide world to find a companion that would love him simply as a cat.

Carol's stomach cramped as she thought of the other possibility. Maybe Romeo's "no" was forever.

But Romeo's kiss was too intoxicating, too full of ineffable bliss to lay aside. She knew that someday, when time had caught back up with her, she would crave that kiss again.

She had time, though. Time to live. Time to love. Time to ask 🐾

Gabriel Beyers was born in Bloomington, Indiana, where he continues to live with his wife, Brandy; young son, Aiden; soon-to-be-born daughter, Olivia; and two dogs, Sammy and Sadie.

"Romeo's Kiss" came from the old-wives'-tale of cats sucking the life from babies as they slept. Originally Romeo was written as an evil cat, and merely saved Carol so that he could have her life for himself. However, the longer he walked around the more he became a powerful yet sad anti-hero longing to live a normal cat's life. Romeo's adventures are far from over, and the old cat is sure to re-surface some day.

Gabriel has spent the last six years learning — and loving — to write, and is now putting the final touches to his first novel, Guarding the Healer.

CATS AND DOGS: AN ESSAY

by H.P. Lovecraft

BEING TOLD of the cat-and-dog fight about to occur in your literary club, I cannot resist contributing a few Thomastic yowls and sibilants upon my side of the dispute, though conscious that the word of a venerable ex-member can scarcely have much weight against the brilliancy of such still active adherents as may bark upon the other side. Aware of my ineptitude at argument, a valued correspondent has supplied me with the records of a similar controversy in the *New York Tribune,* in which Mr. Carl van Doren [a prize-winning biographer] is on my side and Mr. Albert Payson Terhune [a then-famous writer about dogs, especially Collies] on that of the canine tribe. From this I would be glad to plagiarise such data as I need; but my friend, with genuinely Machiavellian subtlety, has furnished me with only a part of the feline section whilst submitting the doggish brief in full. No doubt he imagines that this arrangement, in view of my own emphatic bias, makes for something like ultimate fairness; but for me it is exceedingly inconvenient, since it will force me to be more or less original in several parts of the ensuing remarks.

Between dogs and cats my degree of choice is so great that it would never occur to me to compare the two. I have no active dislike for dogs, any more than I have for monkeys, human beings, tradesmen, cows, sheep, or pterodactyls; but for the cat I have entertained a particular respect and affection ever since the earliest days of my infancy. In its flawless grace and superior self-sufficiency I have seen a symbol of the perfect beauty and bland impersonality of the universe itself, objectively considered; and in its air of silent mystery there resides for me all the wonder and fascination of the unknown. The dog appeals to cheap and facile emotions; the cat, to the deepest founts of imagination and cosmic perception in the human mind. It is no accident that the contemplative Egyptians, together with such later poetic spirits as Poe, Gautier, Baudelaire, and Swinburne, were all sincere worshippers of the supple grimalkin.

Naturally, one's preference in the matter of cats and dogs depends wholly upon one's temperament and point of view. The dog would appear to me to be the favorite of superficial, sentimental, and emotional people — people who feel rather than think, who attach importance to mankind and the popular conventional emotions of the simple, and who find their greatest consolation in the fawning and dependent attachments of a gregarious society. Such people live in a limited world of imagination; accepting uncritically the values of common folklore, and always preferring to have their naïve beliefs, feelings, and prejudices tickled, rather than to enjoy a purely aesthetic and philosophic pleasure arising from discrimination, contemplation, and the recognition of austere, absolute beauty. This is not to say that the cheaper elements do not also reside in the average cat-lover's love of cats, but merely to point out that in ailurophily there exists a basis of true aestheticism which kynophily does not possess. The real lover of cats is one who demands a clearer adjustment to the universe than ordinary household platitudes provide; one who refuses to swallow the sentimental notion that all good people love dogs, children, and horses while all bad people dislike and are disliked by such. He is unwilling to set up himself and his cruder feelings as a measure of universal values, or to allow shallow ethical notions to warp his judgment. In a word, he had rather admire and respect than effuse and dote; and does not fall into the fallacy that pointless sociability and friendliness, or slavering devotion and obedience, constitute anything intrinsically admirable or exalted. Dog-lovers base their whole case on these commonplace, servile, and plebeian qualities, and amusingly judge the intelligence of a pet by its degree of conformity to their own wishes. Cat-lovers escape this delusion; repudiate the idea that cringing subservience and sidling companionship to man are supreme merits; and stand free to worship aristocratic independence, self-respect, and individual personality joined to extreme grace and beauty as typified by the cool, lithe, cynical and unconquered lord of the housetops.

PERSONS of commonplace ideas — unimaginative, worthy burghers who are satisfied with the daily round of things and who subscribe to the popular credo of sentimental values — will always be dog-lovers. To them nothing will ever be more important than themselves and their own primitive feelings, and they will never cease to esteem and glorify the fellow-animal who best typifies these. Such persons are submerged in the vortex of Oriental idealism and abasement which ruined classic civilisation in the Dark Ages, and live in a bleak world of abstract sentimental values wherein the mawkish illusions of meekness, gentleness, brotherhood, and whining humility are magnified into supreme virtues, and a whole false ethic and philosophy erected on the timid reactions of the flexor system of muscles. This heritage, ironically foisted on us when Roman politics raised the faith of a whipped and broken people to supremacy in the later empire, has naturally kept a strong hold over the weak and sentimentally thoughtless; and perhaps reached its culmination in the insipid nineteenth century, when people were wont to praise dogs "because they are so human" (as if humanity were any valid standard of merit!); and honest Edwin Landseer painted hundreds of smug Fidoes and Carlos and Rovers with all the anthropoid triviality, pettiness, and "cuteness "of eminent Victorians.

But amidst this chaos of intellectual and emotional groveling a few free souls have always stood out for the old civilised realities which mediævalism eclipsed — the stern classic loyalty to truth, strength, and beauty given a clear mind and uncowed spirit to the full-living, Western Aryan, confronted by Nature's majesty, loveliness, and aloofness.

This is the virile aesthetic and ethic of the extensor muscles — the bold, buoyant, assertive beliefs and preferences of proud; dominant; unbroken; and unterrified conquerors, hunters, and warriors — and it has small use for the shams and whimperings of the brotherly, affection-slobbering peacemaker and cringer and sentimentalist. Beauty and sufficiency — twin qualities of the cosmos itself — are the gods of this unshackled and pagan type; to the worshipper of such eternal things the supreme virtue will not be found in lowliness, attachment, obedience, and emotional messiness. This sort of worshipper will look for that which best embodies the loveliness of the stars and the worlds and the forests and the seas and the sunsets, and which best acts out the blandness, lordliness, accuracy, self-sufficiency, cruelty, independence, and contemptuous and capricious impersonality of the all governing Nature. Beauty — coolness — aloofness — philosophic repose — self-sufficiency — untamed mastery — where else can we find these things incarnated with even half the perfection and completeness that mark their incarnation in the peerless and softly gliding cat, which performs its mysterious orbit with the relentless and obtrusive certainty of a planet in infinity?

THAT dogs are dear to the unimaginative peasant-burgher whilst cats appeal to the sensitive poet-aristocrat-philosopher will be clear in a moment when we reflect on the matter of biological association.

Practical plebeian folk judge a thing only by its immediate touch, taste, and smell, while more delicate types form their estimates from the linked images and ideas which the object calls up in their minds. Now when dogs and cats are considered, the stolid churl sees only the two animals before him, and bases his favour on their relative capacity to pander to his sloppy, uniformed ideas of ethics and friendship and flattering subservience. On the other hand the gentleman and thinker sees each in all its natural affiliations, and cannot fail to notice that in the great symmetries of organic life dogs fall in with slovenly wolves and foxes and jackals and coyotes and dingoes and painted hyaenas, whilst cats walk proudly with the jungle's lords, and own the haughty lion, the sinuous leopard, the regal tiger, and the shapely panther and jaguar as their kin. Dogs are the hieroglyphs of blind emotion, inferiority, servile attachment, and gregariousness — the attributes of commonplace, stupidly passionate, and intellectually and imaginatively underdeveloped men. Cats are the runes of beauty, invincibility, wonder, pride, freedom, coldness, self-sufficiency, and dainty individuality — the qualities of sensitive, enlightened, mentally developed, pagan, cynical, poetic, philosophic, dispassionate, reserved, independent, Nietzschean, unbroken, civilised, master-class men. The dog is a peasant and the cat is a gentleman. We may, indeed, judge the tone and bias of a civilisation by its relative attitude toward dogs and cats.

THE PROUD Egypt, wherein Pharaoh was Pharaoh and pyramids rose in beauty at the wish of him who dreamed them, bowed down to the cat; and temples were built to its goddess at Bubastis. In imperial Rome the graceful leopard adorned most homes of quality, lounging in insolent beauty in the atrium with golden collar and chain, while after the age of the Antonines the actual cat was imported from Egypt and cherished as a rare and costly luxury. So much for the dominant and enlightened peoples. When, however, we come to the groveling Middle Ages with their

CATS AND DOGS: AN ESSAY

superstitions and ecstasies and monasticisms and maunderings over saints and their relics, we find the cool and impersonal loveliness of the felidae in very low esteem; and behold a sorry spectacle of hatred and cruelty shown toward the beautiful little creature whose mousing virtues alone gained it sufferance amongst the ignorant churls who resented its self-respecting coolness and feared its cryptical and elusive independence as something akin to the dark powers of witchcraft. These boorish slaves of eastern darkness could not tolerate what did not serve their own cheap emotions and flimsy purposes. They wished a dog to fawn and hunt and fetch and carry, and had no use for the cat's gift of eternal disinterested beauty to feed the spirit. One can imagine how they must have resented Pussy's magnificent reposefulness, unhurriedness, relaxation, and scorn for trivial human aims and concernments. Throw a stick, and the servile dog wheezes and pants and stumbles to bring it to you. Do the same before a cat, and he will eye you with coolly polite and somewhat bored amusement. And just as inferior people prefer the inferior animal which scampers excitedly because someone else wants something, so do superior people respect the superior animal which lives its own life and knows that the puerile stick-throwings of alien bipeds are none of its business and beneath its notice. The dog barks and begs and tumbles to amuse you when you crack the whip. That pleases a meekness-loving peasant who relishes a stimulus to his self importance. The cat, on the other hand, charms you into playing for its benefit when it wishes to be amused, making you rush about the room with a paper on a string when it feels like exercise, but refusing all your attempts to make it play when it is not in the humour. That is personality and individuality and self-respect — the calm mastery of a being whose life is its own and not yours — and the superior person recognises and appreciates this because he too is a free soul whose position is assured and whose only law is his own heritage and aesthetic sense.

Altogether, we may see that the dog appeals to those primitive emotional souls whose chief demands on the universe are for meaningless affection, aimless companionship, and flattering attention and subservience; whilst the cat reigns among those more contemplative and imaginative spirits who ask of the universe only the objective sight of poignant, ethereal beauty and the animate symbolisation of Nature's bland, relentless, reposeful, unhurried, and impersonal order and sufficiency. The dog gives, but the cat *is*.

SIMPLE FOLK always overstress the ethical element in life, and it is quite natural that they should extend it to the realm of their pets. Accordingly, we hear many inane dicta in favour of dogs on the ground that they are faithful, whilst cats are treacherous. Now just what does this really mean? Where are the points of reference? Certainly, the dog has so little imagination and individuality that it knows no motives but its master's; but what sophisticated mind can descry a positive virtue in this stupid abnegation of its birthright? Discrimination must surely award the palm to the superior cat, which has too much natural dignity to accept any scheme of things but its own, and which consequently cares not one whit what any clumsy human thinks or wishes or expects of it. It is not treacherous, because it has never acknowledged any allegiance to anything outside its own leisurely wishes; and treachery basically implies a departure from some covenant explicitly recognised. The cat is a realist, and no hypocrite. He takes what pleases him when he wants it, and gives no promises. He never leads you to expect more from him than he gives, and if you choose to be stupidly Victorian enough to mistake his purrs and rubbings of self-satisfaction for marks of transient affection toward you, that is no fault of his. He would not for a moment have you believe that he wants more of you than food and warmth and shelter and amusement — and he is certainly justified in criticising your aesthetic and imaginative development if you fail to find his grace, beauty, and cheerful decorative influence an aboundingly sufficient repayment for all you give him.

The cat-lover need not be amazed at another's love

CATS AND DOGS: AN ESSAY

for dogs — indeed, he may also possess this quality himself; for dogs are often very comely, and as lovable in a condescending way as a faithful old servant or tenant in the eyes of a master — but he cannot help feeling astonished at those who do not share his love for cats. The cat is such a perfect symbol of beauty and superiority that it seems scarcely possible for any true aesthete and civilised cynic to do other than worship it. We call ourselves a dog's "master"— but who ever dared call himself the "master"of a cat? We own a dog — he is with us as a slave and inferior because we wish him to be. But we entertain a cat — he adorns our hearth as a guest, fellow-lodger, and equal because he wishes to be there.

It is no compliment to be the stupidly idolised master of a dog whose instinct it is to idolise, but it is a very distinct tribute to be chosen as the friend and confidant of a philosophic cat who is wholly his own master and could easily choose another companion if he found such a one more agreeable and interesting. A trace, I think, of this great truth regarding the higher dignity of the cat has crept into folklore in the use of the names "cat"and "dog"as terms of opprobrium. Whilst "cat" has never been applied to any sort of offender more than the mildly spiteful and innocuously sly female gossip and commentator, the words "dog" and "cur" have always been linked with vileness, dishonor, and degradation of the gravest type. In the crystallisation of this nomenclature there has undoubtedly been present in the popular mind some dim, half-unconscious realisation that there are depths of slinking, whining, fawning, and servile ignobility which no kith of the lion and the leopard could ever attain. The cat may fall low, but he is always unbroken. He is, like the Nordic among men, one of those who govern their own lives or die.

WE HAVE BUT to glance analytically at the two animals to see the points pile up in favour of the cat. Beauty, which is probably the only thing of any basic significance in all the cosmos, ought to be our chief criterion; and here the cat excels so brilliantly that all comparisons collapse. Some dogs, it is true, have beauty in a very ample degree; but even the highest level of canine beauty falls far below the feline average. The cat is classic whilst the dog is Gothic — nowhere in the animal world can we discover such really Hellenic perfection of form, with anatomy adapted to function, as in the felidae. Puss is a Doric temple — an Ionic colonnade — in the utter classicism of its structural and decorative harmonies. And this is just as true kinetically as statically, for art has no parallel for the bewitching grace of the cat's slightest motion.

THE SHEER, PERFECT aestheticism of kitty's lazy stretchings, industrious face-washings, playful rollings, and little involuntary shiftings in sleep is something as keen and vital as the best pastoral poetry or genre painting; whilst the unerring accuracy of his leaping and springing, running and hunting, has an art-value just as high in a more spirited way but it is his capacity for leisure and repose which makes the cat preëminent. Mr. Carl Van Vechten, in "Peter Whiffle," holds up the timeless restfulness of the cat as a model for life's philosophy, and Prof. William Lyon Phelps has very effectively captured the secret of felinity when he says that the cat does not merely lie down, but "pours his body out on the floor like a glass of water." What other creature has thus merged the aestheticism of mechanics and hydraulics? Contrast this with the inept panting, wheezing, fumbling, drooling, scratching, and general clumsiness of the average dog with his false and wasted motions. And in the details of neatness the fastidious cat is of course immeasurably ahead. We always love to touch a cat, but only the insensitive can uniformly welcome the frantic and humid nuzzlings and pawings of a dusty and perhaps not inodorous canine which leaps and fusses and writhes about in awkward feverishness for no particular reason save that blind nerve-centres have been spurred by certain meaningless stimuli. There is a wearying excess of bad manners in all this doggish fury — well-bred people don't paw and maul one, and surely enough we invariably find the cat gentle and reserved in his advances, and delicate even when he glides gracefully into your lap with cultivated purrs, or leaps whimsically on the table where you are writing to play with your pen in modulated, seriocomic pats. I do not wonder that Mahomet, that sheik of perfect manners, loved cats for their urbanity and disliked dogs for their boorishness; or that cats are the favorites in the polite Latin countries whilst dogs take the lead in heavy, practical, and beer-drinking Central Europe. Watch a cat eat, and then watch a dog. The one is held in check by an inherent and inescapable daintiness, and lends a kind of grace to one of the most ungraceful of all processes. The dog, on the other hand, is wholly repulsive in his bestial and insatiate greediness; living up to his forest kinship of "wolfing" most openly and unashamedly.

RETURNING to beauty of line — is it not significant that while many normal breeds of dogs are conspicuously and admittedly ugly, no healthy and well-developed feline of any species whatsoever is other than beautiful? There are, of course, many ugly cats; but these are always individual cases of mongrelism, malnutrition, deformity, or injury. No breed of cats in its proper condition can by any stretch of the imagination be thought of as even slightly ungraceful — a record against which must be pitted the depressing spectacle of impossibly flattened bulldogs, grotesquely elongated dachshunds, hideously shapeless and shaggy Airedales, and the like. Of course, it may be said that no aesthetic standard is other than relative — but we always work with such standards as we empirically have, and in comparing cats and dogs under the Western European aesthetic we cannot be unfair to either. If any undiscovered tribe in Tibet finds Airedales beautiful and Persian cats ugly, we will not dispute them on their own territory — but just now we are dealing with ourselves and our territory, and here the verdict would not admit of much doubt even from the most ardent kynophile. Such an one usually passes the problem off in an epigrammatic paradox, and says that "Snookums is so homely, he's pretty!" This is the childish penchant for the grotesque and tawdrily "cute" which we see likewise embodied in popular cartoons, freak dolls, and all the malformed decorative trumpery of the "Billikin" or "Krazy Kat" order found in the "dens" and "cosy corners" of the would-be sophisticated yokelry.

IN THE MATTER of intelligence we find the caninites making amusing claims — amusing because they so naïvely measure what they conceive to be an animal's intelligence by its degree of subservience to the human will. A dog will retrieve, a cat will not; therefore (sic!) the dog is the more intelligent. Dogs can be more elaborately trained for the circus and vaudeville acts than cats, therefore (O Zeus, O Royal Mount!) they are cerebrally superior. Now of course this is all the sheerest nonsense. We would not call a weak-spirited man more intelligent than an independent citizen because we can make him vote as we wish whereas we can't influence the independent citizen, yet countless persons apply an exactly parallel argument in appraising the grey matter of dogs and cats. Competition in servility is something to which no self-respecting Thomas or Tabitha ever stooped, and it is plain that any really effective estimate of canine and feline intelligence must proceed from a careful observation of dogs and cats in a detached state — uninfluenced by human beings — as they formulate certain objectives of their own and use their own mental equipment in achieving them. When we do this, we arrive at a very wholesome respect for our purring hearthside friend who makes so little display about his wishes and business methods; for in every conception and calculation he shows a steel-cold and deliberate union of intellect, will, and sense of proportion which puts utterly to shame the emotional sloppings-over and docilely acquired artificial tricks of the "clever" and "faithful" pointer or sheep-dog. Watch a cat decide to move through a door, and see how patiently he waits for his opportunity, never losing sight of his purpose even when he finds it expedient to feign other interests in the interim. Watch him in the thick of the chase, and compare his calculating patience and quiet study of his terrain with the noisy floundering and pawing of his canine rival. It is not often that he returns empty-handed. He knows what he wants, and means to get it in the most effective way, even at the sacrifice of time — which he philosophically recognises as unimportant in the aimless cosmos. There is no turning him aside or distracting his attention — and we know that among humans this is the quality of mental tenacity, this ability to carry a single thread through complex distractions, is considered a pretty good sign of intellectual vigour and maturity. Children, old crones, peasants, and dogs ramble; cats and philosophers stick to their point.

In resourcefulness, too, the cat attests his superiority. Dogs can be well trained to do a single thing, but psychologists tell us that these responses to an automatic memory instilled from outside are of little worth as indices of real intelligence. To judge the abstract development of a brain, confront it with new and unfamiliar conditions and see how well its own strength enables it to achieve its object by sheer reasoning without blazed trails. Here the cats can silently devise a dozen mysterious and successful alternatives whilst poor Fido is barking in bewilderment and wondering what it is all about.

GRANTED that Rover the retriever may make a greater bid for popular sentimental regard by going into the burning house and saving the baby in traditional cinema fashion, it remains a fact that whiskered and purring Nig is a higher-grade biological organism — something physiologically and psychologically nearer a man because of his very freedom from man's orders, and as such entitled to a higher respect from those who judge by purely philosophic and aesthetic standards. We can respect a cat as we cannot respect a dog, no matter which personally appeals the more to our mere doting fancy; and if we be aesthetes and analysts rather than commonplace-lovers and emotionalists, the scales must inevitably turn completely in kitty's favour.

It may be added, moreover, that even the aloof and sufficient cat is by no means devoid of sentimental appeal. Once we get rid of the uncivilised ethical bias — the "treacherous" and "horrid bird-catcher" prejudice — we find in the "harmless cat" the very apex of happy domestic symbolism; whilst small kittens become objects to adore, idealise, and celebrate in the most rhapsodic of dactyls and anapaests, iambics and trochaics. I, in my own senescent mellowness, confess to an inordinate and wholly unphilosophic predilection for tiny coal-black kittens with large yellow eyes, and could no more pass one without petting him than Dr. Johnson could pass a sidewalk post without striking it. There is, likewise, in many cats quite analogous to the reciprocal fondness so loudly extolled in dogs, human beings, horses, and the like.

Cats come to associate certain persons with acts continuously contributing to their pleasure, and acquire for them a recognition and attachment which manifests itself in pleasant excitement at their approach — whether or not bearing food and drink — and a certain pensiveness at their protracted absence.

A CAT with whom I was on intimate terms reached the point of accepting food from no hand but one, and would actually go hungry rather than touch the least morsel from a kindly neighbour source. He also had distinct affections amongst the other cats of that idyllic household; voluntarily offering food to one of his whiskered friends, whilst disputing most savagely the least glance which his coal-black rival "Snowball" would bestow upon his plate. If it be argued that these feline fondnesses are essentially "selfish" and "practical" in their ultimate composition, let us inquire in return how many human fondnesses, apart from those springing directly upon primitive brute instinct, have any other basis. After the returning board has brought in the grand total of zero we shall be better able to refrain from ingenuous censure of the "selfish" cat.

The superior imaginative inner life of the cat, resulting in superior self-possession, is well known. A dog is a pitiful thing, depending wholly on companionship, and utterly lost except in packs or by the side of his master. Leave him alone and he does not know what to do except bark and howl and trot about till sheer exhaustion forces him to sleep. A cat, however, is never without the potentialities of contentment. Like a superior man, he knows how to be alone and happy. Once he looks about and finds no one to amuse him, he settles down to the task of amusing himself; and no one really knows cats without having occasionally peeked stealthily at some lively and well-balanced kitten which believes itself to be alone. Only after such a glimpse of unaffected tail-chasing grace and unstudied purring can one fully understand the charm of those lines which Coleridge wrote with reference to the human rather than the feline young — page eleven:

"... a limber elf,
"Singing, dancing to itself."

But whole volumes could be written on the playing of cats, since the varieties and aesthetic aspects of such sportiveness are infinite. Be it sufficient to say that in such pastimes cats have exhibited traits and actions which psychologists authentically declare to be motivated by genuine humour and whimsicality in its purest sense; so that the task of "making a cat laugh" may not be so impossible a thing even outside the borders of Cheshire.

IN SHORT, a dog is an incomplete thing. Like an inferior man, he needs emotional stimuli from outside, and must set something artificial up as a god and motive. The cat, however, is perfect in himself. Like the human philosopher, he is a self-sufficient entity and microcosm. He is a real and integrated being because he thinks and feels himself to be such, whereas the dog can conceive of himself only in relation to something else. Whip a dog and he licks your hand — frauth! The beast has no idea of himself except as an inferior part of an organism whereof you are the superior part — he would no more think of striking back at you than you would think of pounding your own head when it punishes you with a headache. But whip a cat and watch it glare and move backward hissing in outraged dignity and self-respect! One more blow, and it strikes you in return; for it is a gentleman and your equal, and will accept no infringement on its personality and body of privileges. It is only in your house anyway because it wishes to be, or perhaps even as a condescending favour to yourself. It is the house, not you, it likes; for philosophers realise that human beings are at best only minor adjuncts to scenery. Go one step too far, and it leaves you altogether. You have mistaken your relationship to it and imagined you are its master, and no real cat can tolerate that breach of good manners. Henceforward it will seek companions of greater discrimination and clearer perspective. Let anæmic persons who believe in "turning the other cheek" console themselves with cringing dogs — for the robust pagan with the blood of Nordic twilights in his veins there is no beast like the cat; intrepid steed of Freya, who can boldly look even Thor and Odin full in the face and stare with great round eyes of undimmed yellow or green.

IN THESE OBSERVATIONS I believe I have outlined with some fullness the diverse reasons why, in my opinion and in the smartly timed title-phrase of Mr. Van Doren, "gentlemen prefer cats." The reply of Mr. Terhune in a subsequent issue of the *Tribune* appears to me beside the point; insomuch as it is less a refutation of facts than a mere personal affirmation of the author's membership in that conventional "very human" majority who take affection and companionship seriously, enjoy being important to something alive, hate a "parasite" on mere ethical ground without consulting the right of beauty to exist for its own sake, and therefore love man's noblest and most faithful friend, the perennial dog. I suppose Mr. Terhune loves horses and babies also, for the three go conventionally together in the great hundred-per-center's credo as highly essential likings for every good and lovable he-man of the Arrow Collar and Harold Bell Wright

CATS AND DOGS: AN ESSAY

hero school, even though the automobile and Margaret Sanger have done much to reduce the last two items.

Dogs, then, are peasants and the pets of peasants, cats are gentlemen and the pets of gentlemen. The dog is for him who places crude feeling and outgrown ethic and humanocentricity above austere and disinterested beauty; who just loves "folks and folksiness" and doesn't mind sloppy clumsiness if only something will truly care for him. (Tableau of dog across master's grave — cf. Lanseer, "The Old Shepherd's Chief Mourner.")

The guy who isn't much for highbrow stuff, but is always on the square and don't [sic] often find the [Saturday Evening] Post or the [New York] World too deep for him; who hadn't much use for Valentino, but thinks Doug Fairbanks is just about right for an evening's entertainment. Wholesome — constructive — non-morbid — civic-minded — domestic — (I forgot to mention the radio) normal — that's the sort of go-getter that ought to go in for dogs.

The cat is for the aristocrat — whether by birth or inclinations or both — who admires his fellow-aristocrats. He is for the man who appreciates beauty as the one living force in a blind and purposeless universe, and who worships that beauty in all its forms without regard for the sentimental and ethical illusions of the moment. For the man who knows the hollowness of feeling and the emptiness of human objects and aspirations, and who therefore clings solely to what is real — as beauty is real because it pretends to a significance beyond the emotion which it excites and is. For the man who feels sufficient in the cosmos, and asks no scruples of conventional prejudice, but loves repose and strength and freedom and luxury and sufficiency and contemplation; who as a strong fearless soul wishes something to respect instead of something to lick his face and accept his alternate blows and strokings; who seeks a proud and beautiful equal in the peerage of individualism rather than a cowed and cringing satellite in the hierarchy of fear, subservience, and devolution.

The cat is not for the brisk, self-important little

"worker with a mission," but is for the enlightened, dreaming poet who knows that the world contains nothing really worth doing. The dilettante — the connoisseur — the decadent, if you will; though in a healthier age than this, there were things for such men to do, so that they were the planners and leaders of those glorious, pagan times.

The cat is for him who does things, not for empty duty, but for power, pleasure, splendour, romance, and glamour: for the harpist who sings alone in the night of old battles, or the warrior who goes out to fight such battles for beauty, glory, fame and the splendour of a land athwart which no shadow of weakness falls; for him who will be lulled by no sops of prose and usefulness, but demands for his comfort the ease and beauty and ascendancy and cultivation which make effort worth while; for the man who knows that play, not work, and leisure, not bustle, are the great things of life; and that the round of striving merely in order to strive some more is a bitter irony of which the civilised soul accepts as little as it can.

BEAUTY, sufficiency, ease, and good manners — what more can civilisation require? We have them all in the divine monarch who lounges gloriously on his silken cushion before the hearth. Loveliness and joy for their own sake — pride and harmony and coördination — spirit, restfulness, and completeness — all here are present, and need but a sympathetic disillusionment for worship in full measure. What fully civilised soul but would eagerly serve as high priest of Bast?

The star of the cat, I think, is just now in the ascendant, as we emerge little by little from the dreams of ethics and conformity which clouded the nineteenth century and raised the grubbing and unlovely dog to the pinnacle of sentimental regard.

Whether a renaissance of power and beauty will restore our Western civilisation, or whether the forces of disintegration are already too powerful for any hand to check, none may yet say; but in the present moment of cynical world-unmasking between the pretense of the eighteen-hundreds and the ominous mystery of the decades ahead, we have at least a flash of the old pagan perspective and the old pagan clearness and honesty.

And one idol lit up by that flash, seen fair and lovely on a dream-throne of silk and gold under a chryselephantine dome, is a shape of deathless grace not always given its due among groping mortals — the haughty, the unconquered, the mysterious, the luxurious, the Babylonian, the impersonal, the eternal companion of superiority and art — the type of perfect beauty and the brother of poetry — the bland, grave, compliant, and patrician cat.   🐾

H.P. Lovecraft (1890–1937) also wrote "The Cats of Ulthar," which appeared in the previous Cat Tales *anthology.*

www.ingramcontent.com/pod-product-compliance
Lightning Source LLC
Chambersburg PA
CBHW032204190626
46810CB00018B/1552